Theo Von Marckes

The Franco-German War

Anatiposi

Theo Von Marckes

The Franco-German War

Reprint of the original, first published in 1871.

1st Edition 2023 | ISBN: 978-3-38212-462-5

Anatiposi Verlag is an imprint of Outlook Verlagsgesellschaft mbH.

Verlag (Publisher): Outlook Verlag GmbH, Zeilweg 44, 60439 Frankfurt, Deutschland
Vertretungsberechtigt (Authorized to represent): E. Roepke, Zeilweg 44, 60439 Frankfurt, Deutschland
Druck (Print): Books on Demand GmbH, In de Tarpen 42, 22848 Norderstedt, Deutschland

THE
FRANCO-GERMAN WAR.

A FULL AND GRAPHIC HISTORY

OF THE

GREAT WAR BETWEEN PRUSSIA AND FRANCE,

TOGETHER WITH NUMEROUS

THRILLING AND INTERESTING ANECDOTES, SKETCHES OF THE LIVES OF THE CELEBRATED STATESMEN AND GENERALS ON BOTH SIDES.

BY PROFESSOR THEO. VON MARCKES.

THIS WORK FULLY DIGESTS THE CAUSES LEADING TO THIS MOST REMARKABLE OF
WARS, AND CONTAINS A THOROUGH VENTILATION OF EACH AND EVERY AC-
TION BETWEEN THE RULERS OF BOTH POWERS, MINUTELY DESCRIBING
EVERY BATTLE, AND IN FACT EVERY DETAIL FROM THE MEETING
BETWEEN HIS MAJESTY, KING WILLIAM OF PRUSSIA, AND
COUNT BENEDETTI, FRENCH AMBASSADOR AT EMS, TO THE
SURRENDER OF NAPOLEON III, AND FINALLY
THE ENDING OF THE WAR.

PORTRAITS OF ALL THE GENERALS AND GREAT MEN,
AND MANY OTHER FINE ILLUSTRATIONS.

PHILADELPHIA:
PUBLISHED BY BARCLAY & CO.,
610 ARCH STREET.

THE FRANCO-GERMAN WAR.

PRUSSIA and France have, for some years past, been APPARENTLY peacefully disposed towards each other. There are not so many causes leading to this war as Napoleon would have the world at large to believe. When the nomination of Prince Leopold, as King of Spain, was withdrawn, the Emperor lost an available excuse for war ; but the clamor in France for war grew louder and louder, and war was *certain* because "France wanted it."

The outcry at first seemed to be confined to the ministerial organs of Paris ; but as these became peaceable in their tone, the more independent organs grew warlike, and Napoleon having, as he supposed, stimulated public opinion to back him, stood prepared to plunge into the contest.

The Emperor of the French had no further excuse for war, unless, indeed, that Prussia had been biting her thumb at him ; but if the French people believe, with CAPULET'S SERVANT, that biting of thumbs is a "disgrace to them if they bear it," this, no doubt, proves to them a sufficient excuse.

While Napoleon had been reaching this resolution, not only had his cause been growing weaker, but his difficulties were increased, and he stood before the world in the attitude of a man who having first threatened war for an *inadequate* cause, finds even that cause taken from him, and then exclaims, "Never mind, I will fight, anyhow." His adversary, on the other hand, had conciliated respect by a firm and dignified bearing, a courage without *bluster*, a resolution without undue obstinacy.

By this calm and collected attitude, Prussia had, moreover, gained material advantages. She compelled France to expose clearly her purpose of seizing the Rhenish frontier, and thus stimulated the patriotism of the non-confederated German provinces, which could not then hesitate to join the Confederation with all their available force. She thus gained time to complete her preparations for the defence of the Rhine. This was an advantage of the very utmost importance. The whole frontier is a network of fortresses, upon which Prussia for years past has been lavishing money and exhausting the ingenuity of engineers. The true policy of an invading force would have been to fall upon them suddenly, but the time for this has passed, "and the besieger found himself *besieged*."

Napoleon the First often remarked, "A military blunderer is worse than a traitor," and the Napoleon of to-day is not like the first Napoleon, because he lacks military experience, because he lacks conciseness ; in fact, to sum it all up, "he's alike, and yet not alike."

Napoleon maintained his threatening attitude toward Prussia, and persisted in his offensive demands, and all the efforts of that country at explanation were not accepted.

Throughout the whole affair, the attitude of France was that of an enraged ruffian, bent upon insult. To be sure, the attitude of Prussia was calculating and somewhat exasperating, but she has decidedly the advantage thus far in the quarrel.

The pretext which France has used to produce a conflict upon which Napoleon has fixed his heart for a long time past is removed. We now see that France has discovered that, after all, it is the Rhine frontier which she wants, and for which she proposes to do battle. Prince Leopold withdrew from the nomination as King of Spain, ("What's in a name?") because, as stated, he did not wish to involve Prussia in a bloody, and, perhaps, protracted war. Before going farther we will give the exact history of the

MEETING BETWEEN THE KING OF PRUSSIA AND BENEDETTI, FRENCH AMBASSADOR.

We make a simple record of facts from official documents :

The first meeting took place at Ems, on the 9th of July, at the request of Count Benedetti. It was demanded by him that the King should require the Prince of Hohenzollern to withdraw his acceptance of the Spanish Crown. The King replied that, as in the whole affair, he had been addressed only as the head of the family, and never as the King of Prussia, and had accordingly given no command for the acceptance of the candidature, he could also give no command for withdrawal. On the 11th of July Count Benedetti requested a second audience, which was granted. In this interview he was urgent with the King to prevail upon Prince Leopold to renounce the crown. The King replied, that the Prince was perfectly free to decide for himself, and that, moreover, he did not even know where he was at that moment, as he was about to take a journey among the Alps. On the morning of July 13, the King met Benedetti on the public promenade before the fountain, and gave him an extra sheet of *The Cologne Gazette*, which he had just received, with a private telegram from Sigmaringen, relating the withdrawal of the Prince, remarking at the same time that he himself had heard nothing from Sigmaringen, but should expect letters that day. Count Benedetti replied that he had already received the information the evening before from Paris, and as the King regarded the matter as thus settled, the Count wholly unexpectedly made a new demand, proposing to the King that he should expressly pledge himself never to give his consent in case the question of the candidature should at any subsequent time be revived. The King decidedly refused to comply with any such demand, and when Benedetti returned to his proposal with increasing importunity, stood by his answer. In spite of this, a few hours after, the Count requested a third audience. Upon being asked what subject was to be considered, he gave for answer that he wished to renew the discussion of the morning. The King declined another audience, as he had no answer but that already given, and, moreover, all negotiations must now take place through the Ministry. Benedetti requested permission to take leave of the King, upon his departure from Ems, which was so far granted that the King bowed to him as the latter was leaving the railway station the next day for Coblenz. Each of the interviews of Benedetti with the King had the character of a private conversation. The Count did not once pretend to be acting in his official capacity.

In the preceding statement, which is sanctioned by the King himself, no mention is made of the rudeness of Benedetti in forcing himself upon His Majesty while indulging in the recreation of a walk on the crowded promenade of Ems. It was generally regarded, however, as a studied insult on the part of the French Minister, and was commented on with indignation by the German press. Such a violation of diplomatic courtesy could hardly have been accidental. Not even the excitement of a sudden surprise could excuse the incivility; but there was no surprise in the case; the Count had received the news the night before, and had at least twelve hours to meditate his course of action. The affair was witnessed with astonishment by the numerous spectators of the scene, who drew their own augury of its probable consequences. It was interpreted as a sign of hostility toward Prussia, and two days after came the declaration of war.

In spite of the seriousness of the occasion,

the procedure had a certain comic side, which is thus described by an eye-witness: "On Wednesday morning the King was taking his usual walk on the promenade, among the other visitors at Ems, in the company of two or three gentlemen. Happening to turn my head, I saw that the King had been fastened upon by a short, fat figure, who was gesticulating and talking with the utmost animation. I asked the bystanders who was that little man in the light-brown summer dress, with his hair cut close to the head, but could get no satisfaction. His liveliness struck me as very strange, it formed such a contrast to the quiet manners of the King, and I could not help following his movements with my eye. The conversation did not continue much longer; the King spoke a few words mildly to the little Italian, as I took him to be, made a parting motion with his hand and his hat, and pursued his way to the house where he lodged. The little man snatched off his hat in a hurry, turned on his heel, and feeling in his breast-pocket, drew out a paper which he gave to one of the gentlemen that accompanied the King. And this little pepper-pot, as I afterward learned, was not an Italian, but a Corsican, and his name was Benedetti."

The final communication with the French Ambassador was through Prince Radziwill, an adjutant in the personal suit of the King, who has since given a detailed account of the interview. "In consequence of a conversation with Count Benedetti on the promenade, on the morning of July 13," says he, "I was commanded by the King, about two o'clock in the afternoon, to take the following message to the Count: 'His Majesty has received within an hour, a written communication from Prince Hohenzollern, fully confirming the intelligence in regard to the withdrawal of Prince Leopold from the Spanish candidature, which the Count had received directly from Paris. The King regarded this as a final settlement of the question.' After I had delivered this message to Count Benedetti, he replied that since his conversation with the King, he had received a new dispatch from the Duke de Gramont, in which he was instructed to request an audience of the King, and lay before him once more the wishes of the French Government. 1. That he should approve the withdrawal of Prince Hohenzollern. 2. That he should give the assurance that the same candidature should never be again accepted in the future. Hereupon His Majesty commanded me to reply to the Count that he approved of the withdrawal of Prince Leopold in the same sense, and to the same extent, as he had previously approved of his acceptance. The written communication which he had received was from Prince Anton of Hohenzollern (father of Leopold), who had been authorized thereto by prince Leopold himself. In respect to the second point, assurance for the future, His Majesty could only refer to what he had said to the Count in the morning. Count Benedetti received this reply of the King with thanks, and said that he would announce it to his Government, as he was authorized to do. In regard to the second point, however, he was obliged, by the express instructions in the last dispatch of the Duke de Gramont, to request another conversation with the King, if it were only to hear a repetition of the same words, especially as new arguments were contained in the last dispatch, which he would like to present to His Majesty. Upon this, at about half past five o'clock, after dinner, the King ordered me to reply for the third time to Count Benedetti, that he must decidedly decline any further discussion of the last point, relating to a guarantee for the future. What he had said in the morning was his final word on that subject, and he could only refer to that. Upon being assured that the arrival of Count Bismarck in Ems the next day was not certain, Count Benedetti remarked that for his part he would content himself with the declaration of the King."

The actual demands of the French Government upon the King are contained in a subsequent dispatch from Baron Werther, the Prussian Minister at Paris. In a conversation with the Duke de Gramont, the latter remarked that he regarded the withdrawal of Prince Leopold as a matter of secondary importance, but he feared that the course of Prussia in regard to it would occasion a permanent misunderstanding between the two countries. It was necessary to guard against this by destroying the germ. The conduct of Prussia toward France had been unfriendly. This was admitted, to his certain knowledge, by all the great powers. To speak frankly, he did not wish for war, but would rather preserve amicable relations with Prussia. He hoped that Prussia had similar dispositions. He was satisfied with the intentions of the Prussian Minister, and they could, accordingly, freely discuss the conditions of reconciliation. He would suggest the writing of a letter to the Emperor by the King, disavowing all purpose of infringing upon the interests or the dignity of France in his authorizing the acceptance of the Spanish crown by Prince Leopold. The King should confirm the withdrawal of the Prince, and express the hope that all ground of complaint between the two Governments would thus be removed. Nothing should be said in the letter concerning the family relations between Prince Leopold and the Emperor.

The refusal of the King to accept the humiliating conditions proposed by the French Government called forth the liveliest approval and sympathy in all parts of Germany. It awakened a deep feeling of affection for his person, confidence in his judgment, and devotion to his interests. He is now identified not only with the rights of Prussia, but with the cause of German unity, and the defence of German honor.

The day after his final and eventful interview with Benedetti, the King left Ems at an early hour in the morning in a special train for Berlin. He took leave of the crowd which had assembled to witness his departure with evident emotion. "I hope to see you all once more," said he. "God is my witness that I have not desired war; but if I am forced into it, I will maintain the honor of Germany to the last man."

His journey was like a triumphal progress. The heartfelt greetings with which he was received by the people on the way indicate the sentiment of the whole population. Never, in the history of the world, did a sovereign enjoy such enthusiastic approval from his subjects for an official act. The feeling is spontaneous and universal. Upon his arrival at Coblenz, he was received by a military corps, called the "War Union," with music and banners. He could only say: "My comrades, I rejoice greatly in the surprise which you have prepared for me."

At Cassel, the capital of the new Prussian province of Hesse, he was welcomed by the authorities of the city, and a large concourse of people. In a brief speech he expressed his satisfaction at finding such patriotic sentiments in the new capital, and continued his journey amid shouts of congratulations. He arrived in Berlin, or rather at the Potsdam station, about nine o'clock in the evening. The streets were alive with throngs of people who had come to bid him welcome home. Every spot in the vicinity was full. Prussian banners and German flags waved from all the windows. Many of the houses were illuminated. The carriages were not allowed to pass in the street, but were drawn up, full of people, in long lines on each side. The waiting-room of the King at the station was covered with banners, and filled with garlands and wreaths of fresh flowers. Among the crowd were many military officers of the highest rank, the civil authorities of the city, the most eminent merchants and bankers, and a host of ladies in full dress. The great mass of the population of Berlin appeared to be present, and the streets were so completely blocked up that it was almost impossible to pass. At three o'clock the Crown Prince, Count Bismarck, the Minister of War, Gen. Roon and Gen. Moltke, had gone to meet the King at Brandenburg. It was there that the King first heard of the declaration of war, and immediately gave orders for mobilizing the army. The train was signaled at a quarter before nine, and entered the station amid shouts of welcome. As the King left the carriage he gave his hand to Field Marshal Wrangel, who imprinted upon it a reverent kiss. He was deeply moved by his reception. Advancing slowly along the platform, he reached his hand to the right and left, bowing to the multitude as he passed, and receiving the bouquets which were showered upon him by the ladies.

He was now greeted by the representative of the City Government, who pledged himself for the devotion and self-sacrifice of the people. The King replied in a few words of good cheer. After a short time, the King got into a carriage, with the Crown Prince, and drove from the station amid thunders of applause. The whole way to the palace was one act of homage. There was not a word nor a look of anxiety among that innumerable host. Not a breath betrayed a feeling of doubt. Every soul was inspired with trust in God and a good cause. All was confidence and congratulation, if not joy. As the carriage approached the palace, the pressure became so great that even the stone pillars in the public square broke as if they had been made of wood. The ceaseless hurras roared like a hurricane around the place. The King alighted on the steps, and with deep emotion repeatedly expressed his thanks. He could scarcely be heard for the acclamations, but those who stood nearest to him caught the words : "With such inspiration of my people, our victory is secure; we may look forward to the future without fear." The King then entered the palace, but the crowd remained. All at once, the national hymn began to ascend from ten thousand voices. The people stood with uncovered heads. A small proportion only were able to sing; the others wept from excitement; and even those who took part in the hymn could do so only with trembling voice and tearful eye. It was a moment of sublime transfiguration. A little before 11 o'clock, Gen. Moltke made his appearance in the square. He was received with a storm of welcome, and the people could hardly be restrained from taking him on their shoulders, and bearing him into the palace. At length, about half an hour before midnight, the multitude were informed that the King had still many heavy tasks to attend to, and begged them to retire. "Home! Home!" was at once, the universal cry, and in a few minutes the vast throng had disappeared, and left not a soul in the spacious square.

In other parts of the town, the excitement continued till nearly morning. An address to the King was hastily extemporized, taken to the nearest printing office, and soon distributed among the people. It was somewhat to this effect : "In this time of danger, when the honor of Prussia, of Germany, is boldly outraged by French audacity, when security and peace are causelessly and criminally threatened, your people are impelled to express their unshakable fidelity, and their universal enthusiasm for the fight. As in 1813–'15, around your Majesty's noble father, every Prussian, with blood and treasure, will now stand around your glorious leaders in the war. Only one thing have your faithful people to supplicate of your Majesty, never to rest until this French arrogance shall be humbled for all time, and Germany restored to its ancient greatness. Only one word have we to speak : With God for King and Fatherland! Hurrah! Hurrah!"

The signatures to this address soon amounted to many thousands.

It was reported, and by many believed, that the French army would at once make a "promenade" through the south of Germany. The delay gave an unexpected time for preparation to the German forces. There have been many strangers here from America and England, who have been tempted by the beauty of the environs, the healthfulness of the climate, and the advantages for education, to select Stuttgart as a place of temporary residence. But they are now more desirous to go away than they have ever been to come. Prices have gone up with a bound, and business is at a stand-still. Credit is greatly disturbed, and travellers find it difficult to obtain cash for their drafts on the greatest Parisian bankers. There is no telegraph to France or Switzerland, no trains to the north or west, and letters to America go only by way of England. Even the mails are suspended from Frankfort to France. The people here take the situation quietly. Families are ordered to be in readiness for the quartering of 16,500 troops. at the rate of six to ten to a family. Fine carriage horses are taken out of their stables for the uses of the Government at a nominal price. But the spirit of the people is undaunted, and will not easily quail, even before the terrors of machine cannon and chassepôts.

We now come to the date made memorial by the

UPRISING OF THE GERMAN PEOPLE.

(From our own correspondent.)

STUTTGART, July 25.—It is now evident that the war declared by Louis Napoleon against Prussia is to be fought with the entire German race. Munich, Stuttgart, and Baden are glowing with a patriotic ardor no less fervent than that which inspires the population of Berlin. The distinctions of party, as well as those of nationality, are lost in the prevailing enthusiasm. With few exceptions, the hostility to Prussia, which was called forth by the events of '66, has subsided, and the ancient German feeling has regained possession of every heart. Even the Democrats and Socialists, who are bitter enemies of the Prussian monarchy, and with whom Bismarck is the object of supreme abhorrence, have laid aside their feuds, and are flocking to the common standard for the defence of the Fatherland. The country now presents a glorious spectacle. There have been few such moments in history. Even the stranger in the land cannot withhold his sympathy and admiration from the spirit which pervades the people.

The first announcement of the war was the signal for a universal burst of patriotic feeling. There was no hesitation, no shrinking, no distrust. Personal interests were at once postponed to the cause of the country. The war was accepted as an inevitable necessity,—a war not of conquest, not of ambi-

EMPEROR NAPOLEON.

Kaiser Napoleon.

EMPRESS EUGENIE.

Kaiserin Eugenie.

tion, not of political intrigue—but a war for the protection of the fireside, and of the native soil. In Berlin, there was but one voice of devotion to the King, and assurance of victory. "Come what may," was the general cry, "we cannot be conquered by the French." "At first, it may go hard with us," said one of the aged merchants of the city, "we may lose a great battle, we have no pledge of the fortune of war, and the French are a powerful enemy; but we must and shall be victorious; even if the children from school, and old men like myself, are called to take part in the conflict." There was great excitement on the Bourse, but not a tongue was raised against the war. It was announced that 950,000 men were at the disposal of Prussia, of whom nearly 700,000 were ready to take the field. The army of Saxony was at once put in motion; Dresden and Leipsic joined hands with Berlin; and even from the newly annexed provinces of Prussia, not a discordant note was heard. It was said in Darmstadt: "Let Germany fearlessly take up the gage that has been thrown down, and follow the lead of Prussia into the fight; for our cause is just, and Heaven will be on our side." In Hanover, the war with France was hailed with acclamation. In the places of public amusement, which were filled with people, the enthusiasm was so great as to put a stop to the performances. Nothing would do but patriotic songs. "Des Deutschen Vaterland," (the German Fatherland) "Die Wacht am Rhein," (the Watch on the Rhine) and even "Das Preussenlied," (the Prussian Song) were repeatedly called for and loudly echoed by the crowded audiences.

The expressions of feeling in Southern Germany were equally prompt and decisive. The largest public meeting that was ever known in Stuttgart, was held on the Saturday evening after the reception of the news. Every political party was represented, and all spoke with one voice in favor of the war. There was no question that Würtemberg would join heart and hand in the common cause. The mobilizing of the army commenced without delay, and numbers of the young men of the city came forward as volunteers. Here is no dodging of military duty, no creeping away under some plea of exemption; everybody who is able is willing to serve; and those who cannot, pour out their money like water. In Tübingen, that old University town, famed for the choice variety of theological opinion which it dispenses to every taste, a great public gathering assembled on Sunday evening. The crowd was so immense that it was necessary to adjourn from a hall of the Museum to the spacious riding-school. It was urged upon the Government to take vigorous measures for the prosecution of the war, which was pronounced essential to the existence of the nation, and the security of every household. Every true German could now have but one motto: "Against France to the last man,

and to the last breath." Tübingen will suffer from the war more than many large towns in Germany. The news came upon her like a bomb-shell. The University is her main dependence, and the students are now leaving almost in a body. Many of them are from North Germany, and must go at once. The subjects of military duty from Würtemberg reported themselves at once, a part of them as ready to march.

The German watering-places feel the effect of the sudden change severely. More than 2,000 persons left Ems in a single day. There was such a rush at the railway station that the police were obliged to keep order with drawn swords. The French, who were leaving, tied white pocket-handkerchiefs to their canes and umbrellas. Baden-Baden, as well as the resorts of less note in the Black Forrest, are quite deserted. Most of the hotels are entirely empty, and waiters are summoned to exchange their white waistcoats for a military uniform.

The personal narrative of a visitor at Creuznach, may give an idea of the experience of many of the German Summer travellers:

"On Thursday morning," says he, "when the renunciation of Prince Leopold appeared to have settled the question, certainly for the present, I started from Frankfort, and arriving at Wiesbaden, found the watering-place life still in full bloom. The gardens were filled with a throng of gay persons, players sat around the green table, there was music on the promenade, and the different places of interest in the vicinity were alive with elegant equipages. It was on the journey through the Rheingau, that I first heard of the prostration of our hopes for peace. In Creuznach, where I arrived on Friday, the 15th, the effects were already to be seen. A great number of strangers had left in the morning, and during the day the stations from Münster to Creuznach were besieged with crowds of passengers. Even lame men on crutches and children were brought in all sorts of vehicles, to the train. Still the public garden presented its usual appearance in the evening. There was music in the brilliantly-lighted pavilion; a great concourse of people, mostly in rich toilets, filled the seats and walks, and gayly-dressed children were playing on the lawn. On Saturday morning we heard of the declaration of war from an extra of the Creuznach *Gazette*. An excursion at 10 o'clock, in the vicinity of the Rhine, brought us into the midst of military preparations. The trains were delayed at every station. Everywhere our path was crossed by long rows of locomotives coupled together, and cars filled with troops and munitions of war. Every station was crowded as full as it could hold with people from the neighborhood, to hear the news. Upon our return to Creuznach, what a contrast to last evening! No music was heard in the pavilion—only the melancholy tones of a little bell on the neighboring church.

The throng of fashionables that make up the society of a watering-place had dwindled to a very few persons. These sat together without speaking, each preoccupied with his own serious thoughts. The thriving town of hotels and boarding-houses, which, in a single generation, had taken the place of rude wooden hovels, had suddenly become desolate. The showy shops stood without a purchaser, the boatmen were thrown out of employment, although the walls were still covered with placards announcing regattas and fireworks, and illuminations. Servants were lounging idly around, and the carriage-drivers had nothing to do but to take strangers to the railway. On Sunday morning the town of Creuznach was completely isolated by the suspension of all the trains, and at the same time, the horses from every part of the circle were mustered into the army.

"In the North of Germany generally, the excitement was no less intense than in Berlin. The Chief Magistrate of Schleswig-Holstein, upon his accession to office, calls upon the people for their aid to the war: 'My first official duty among you,' he says, 'falls in a difficult, but still an exalting time. I had hoped to labor with you in the peaceful building up of our common country. But the Almighty has ordered it otherwise. A sudden and outrageous attack has been made upon the honor of our nation. The hereditary enemy of our Fatherland has declared war upon us without cause. Armed hosts already press upon our borders. The whole army, the whole people, is summoned to arms. Every one rushes to the banners with alacrity and joy. No man will hold back. Our natural allies, the South-German States, stand true to us. Let us, then, look forward to the great conflict with devotion and trust in God. We know that when a people defends its honor and its right against an insolent foe, when it cheerfully sacrifices its blood and its treasure to the holy cause of its country, then God the Lord will take them under His protection.' Schleswig-Holstein has hitherto been torn by parties. Now there is no feeling but that of perfect unity. The Central Committee of the Liberal party issues an address, breathing a spirit of the loftiest patriotism:

"Men of Schleswig-Holstein! The decision is made. France breaks over the German Rhine. Germany stands ready with every sacrifice to meet the foe. In long, hard fights, even when all had left us, have we defended every foot of the German soil. What duty and honor require stand written in every German breast. The children of our land will fight in the front ranks. Onward, then, to the combat, for Germany united in freedom and might, and may God bless our righteous weapons."

In the city of Bremen, there prevailed the highest degree of enthusiasm. As soon as France drew the sword, you heard expressions of confidence at the corner of every street. The young men hastened joyfully to the banners. Patriotic fathers telegraphed to their sons in America to come home. The wives bore the message of young exempts in that country, who would not use their privilege, when their Fatherland was attacked. Although trade in Bremen is at an end, navigation broken off, and millions of money at risk on the event, there is but one sentiment of manly resistance to the enemy. All the buoys and signals at the mouth of the Weser have been sunk, or removed to prevent the entrance of the French iron-clads that have sailed from Cherbourg. It is supposed that they are driving for the harbors of the North Sea, in order to make a descent upon Schleswig-Holstein. The news from Bavaria and Würtemberg, of the preparations for war, was received with high exultation in Bremen.

The same feeling was manifested in Lubeck. On the Sunday, after war was declared, more than 20,000 people assembled in a large field before the gates of the city. An inspiriting address was made, responding to the feelings of every German heart, at the close of which every man in the vast multitude, with uncovered head, and hands raised to heaven, solemnly pledged himself to defend his country with his blood. Nearly a hundred young men from Frankfort and the vicinity, who had served out their regular time in the army, and had gone to England as clerks in mercantile houses, have returned as volunteers, and have been mustered into the service. They received great sympathy from their acquaintances in England, as well as on their passage through Belgium, and their employers have promised to keep their places for them against their return.

The Crown Prince of Prussia arrived at Stuttgart, July 28, about 8 o'clock, on his way to the frontier, to take command of the South German army. He was received with an enthusiastic welcome by the people. Every street in the vicinity of the station, where he alighted, was crowded. A long line stood on each side as he passed with his suite. They drove in several carriages to the royal palace, where he is to stop for a short time. This was a great day in Stuttgart. Large bodies of soldiers, in complete warlike equipment, were constantly marching through the town on their way to the frontier. They had the appearance of stout, hardy men, inured to labor and fatigue, and the alacrity of their movements was truly animating.

Up to this time nothing of moment appears to have occurred. There had been several slight rencontres between the soldiers on each side, and alarms were sufficiently frequent to keep the Prussians on the alert. Under date of Tuesday, July 19, it was announced from Saarbruck (one of the chief points on the Prussian frontier opposite Forbach, a small village in the French territory), that constant excitement prevailed. The approach of the French was expected every hour. The garrison was fully prepared to give them a warm reception. The day before, in the afternoon, a peasant brought the information that the French were seen on the heights of Forbach. A company immediately marched at double-quick toward the place. At the same time, a troop of uhlans pushed on from St. Johann on the Saar to the French lines. The remainder of the garrison took their stand opposite to the railway bridge. It was an exciting moment. All the shops were shut. The women and children took refuge in the cellars. Every instant it was expected that the battle would begin in the streets. But it turned out to be a false alarm. The troops returned about 5 o'clock without having seen an enemy. At 3 o'clock the next morning the general march was again beat. Officer after officer rode rapidly through the streets. Soon the uhlans were on the move, while the entrances to the principal streets were guarded by infantry. This time it was not a false alarm.

FIRST SIGHT OF THE ENEMY.

On a wooded height before the town the uhlans received several squadrons of French chasseurs. They went at them with loud hurrahs, but the chasseurs, after firing two or three shots, rode off in a hurry within their own lines. The uhlans had no orders to pursue them, and returned to their quarters. The shot hit the horse of one of the officers on the hind leg, but no other damage was done.

The first French blood spilled was on the next day, Wednesday, July 20, when one of the French patrols was shot by a corporal of the Prussian advance guard. The body of the soldier was left on the spot by the chasseurs, as they fled, and was afterward buried near by. It was remarked, as a noticeable coincidence, that the shot was fired by a soldier of the so-called Hohenzollern regiment. On the afternoon of the same day, a chasseur was shot by a Prussian sergeant, and the whole number of killed on the French side amounts to eight, one of them a mounted infantry officer, who fell dead from his horse. The French are bad shots. They blaze away as soon as they see a soldier's cap, though there is only one. The Chassepôts carry to a long distance, but do not hit well. Only two Prussians have been wounded, and those slightly. The French are found in considerable numbers in the woods on the left bank of the Saar. They kept cracking away with their guns, and the laborers in the vicinity are obliged to quit work. A ball occasionally strikes a train returning from Saar Louis. The French people on the lines are in a state of great depression, showing a strong contrast to the buoyant spirit that prevails everywhere in Germany. All the manufactories are shut up, and thousands of workmen are thrown out of employment.

Since the above writing, I have received two days later reports. Early on Saturday morning (July 23), a battalion of French infantry attempted to get possession of the bridge at Wehrden. The commandant of the fort at Saar Louis sent out a battalion of infantry and a squadron of uhlans, who soon drove them back. About 7 o'clock the French soldiers made a descent upon the railway bridge at Schaunenberge, but were repulsed after a brisk fire on both sides.

Below we give the names and character of the iron-clads in the navies of Prussia and France :

PRUSSIA.	
Broadside.	*Turret.*
Konig Wilhelm.	Arminius.
Kron Prinz.	Prince Adalbert.
Renown.	And 2 building.

FRANCE.	
Broadside.	*Broadside.*
Magenta.	Magnanime.
Solferino.	Rochambeau.
Gloire.	Devastation.
Invincible.	Congreve.
Normandie.	Lave.
Couronne.	Foudroyante.
Provence.	*Turret.*
Heroine.	Foudroyante.
Savoir.	Taureau.
Revanche.	Belliqueuse.
Surveilliante.	Belier.
Flandre.	Boule Dogue.
Guyeuse.	Cerbere.
Gauloise.	And twenty floating
Valeureuse.	batteries.

THE SENTIMENT OF FRANCE.

SCENE IN THE FRENCH CORPS LEGISLATIF—PRO-TESTS AGAINST THE WAR—POSITION OF THE LIB-ERALS.

The first glimpse of the true history of the declaration of war was obtained from the Paris papers of July 17th, containing the report of Friday's debate in the Corps Législatif. After the Duc de Gramont's declaration, a demand was made for the dispatches. Ollivier, after refusing to give them, was compelled to admit that France had finally declared war on account of the Prussian dispatch communicating to the European Courts the King's refusal to receive the French Ambassador ; and that this dispatch, thus made the basis of war, had not been seen by any French Minister. The Government had, in fact, declared war on what purported to be an abstract of that dispatch, supplied by two French spies, whose names were withheld.

When war was announced the Left refused to join in the shouts of the majority. When the majority voted an extra war credit of 500,000,000 francs, the Left again sat silent. The majority, thereupon, began a vehement altercation.

M. Thiers said : When such a demonstration is made, I wish to say why I did not rise with the majority. I believe I love my country. If there was ever a solemn day it is this. When war shall be declared nobody will grant to Government more readily than I the means of conquering. My patriotism equals yours. We are considering a declaration of war made by the ministry of the tribune. Does such a declaration concern the ministry alone, not us? Our duty is to reflect. The resolution you have just adopted is the death of thousands of men. One instant, I beseech you, of reflection! Bethink you of May 8, 1866. You refused then to hear me when I sought to show you what was about to happen. Let that recollection persuade you to listen now. The principal demand of Government has been conceded; [Interruption] my conscience tells me I fulfil a duty in resisting imprudent passions, and representing soberly the country's interests. Is this a time for you to break the peace on a mere question of susceptibility? You are shedding torrents of blood for question of form. I ask for the dispatches upon which resolution for war has been adopted. If I had the honor to govern my country, I should have wished to give it time for reflection. I regard this war as an imprudence, and its occasion as ill-chosen. More than anybody else, I desire reparation for 1866. No doubt Prussia has deceived us. [Interruption.] You do not understand that I discharge the most painful duty of my life. I pity you; insult me if you will; I will endure everything; but you do not fulfil your whole duty, and that is why I call for the dispatches.

M. Ollivier, briefly replying, refused the dispatches absolutely.

M. Gambetta renewed the demand, saying: "You put the responsibility of war on a dispatch; you must show us the dispatch."

M. Ollivier.—"I will read two dispatches, but not the signatures, for our agents would be sent away." M. Ollivier then read part of one dispatch, confirming the refusal of King William to receive the French Ambassador, and two dispatches from French agents abroad, giving the substance of Bismarck's circular. The circular itself, M. Ollivier did not pretend to produce. He concluded by saying: "We go to war with a light heart, and confident in our army."

After an interval and other questions, M. Ollivier said; "We will tell the whole truth: What we could not endure was the semi-official communication to all Europe of the rejection of our Ambassador, all the more significant because done in the most courteous terms." "The right," says La Liberté, a vehement war organ, "received M. Ollivier's speech with consternation." M. Thiers attempted to reply, but was interrupted.

M. Duvernois.—War is due to Cabinet blunder.

M. Thiers.—It is to a blunder that we owe war. M. Ollivier has evaded the question. Prussia ought to have been attacked when she desired to unite the German States; then war would have been legitimate, and we should have been sustained. I blamed Sadowa at the time; to-day the world demands legitimate complaints. Prussia also has committed a great fault in negotiating with Spain; yet Prussia wished peace, and

we have war. If we had still to require the renunciation of the Hohenzollern candidature, I should be with you, but now that we have obtained that, we demand something else. You had not only obtained your result; you had form and substance both; yet you say Prussia has not yielded in form, and we have been insulted. Public opinion will turn against us; the journals of Europe will be against us. Prussia never would have resumed this candidature. It would have been madness.

Duc de Gramont.—Why, then, did she not promise?

M. Arago.—Because you challenged her.

M. Thiers.—She refused because you began all. I know well that I shock your feelings, but I know there is the heart of the question. I have heard my opinions echoed on all sides.

Great clamors here arose, and M. Thiers, in reply to the interruptions, declared that "he would only yield the tribune to violence." He then resumed: We no longer live in the peace-at-any-price times; to demand war at any price is the servility of a courtier. But I am of no party.

M. David accused Thiers of wanting patriotism and bringing misfortune upon France. [Cries of "Order!" on the Left.]

M. Thiers.—Misfortune upon France! It is not I who have caused it. It is they who would not listen to our warnings, you who voted Mexico and Sadowa. Had you but permitted us to discuss now under a liberal regime, would you refuse to hear me? You shall not hinder me from speaking: my duty is to pour light on a great fault.

Nothing could be so significant as such a speech from Thiers, who has constantly shown a jealous dislike of Prussia, a readiness for war on any reasonable pretext, and a belief that France ought to do as she likes in Europe. *Not one word of this speech was allowed to reach England by telegraph.* There has been a systematic effort to deceive Europe about public opinion in France respecting war, and to deceive France about the opinions of Europe. Telegrams to English papers during the past week have misrepresented the tone of the French independent press, and suppressed the manifestations against war. The French telegrams declared that the French press was all for war. This is true only of the Government organs. The *Débats, Temps, Rappel, Siècle, Reveil* and *Cloche* are all strongly opposed to it. The most eminent Republican leaders were for peace! Louis Blanc, in the *Temps* and *Rappel,* protested with matchless vigor and ability against this last imperial crime. Even journals like the *Figaro,* mere organs of what is popular to-day, have given but doubtful support to the Government. An immense majority of the provincial journals resisted war. The demonstrations on the Boulevard were police work; the students took little part in what was attributed to them. A letter in *Rappel* shows that the disposition of the Liberal party, as a whole, throughout France is against the war, but they can no longer oppose it. Popular or not in its origin, the war fever runs high for the moment, and not even the French exiles want to see France beaten. Telegrams to the French papers similarly misrepresented the English press. Some journals at the beginning were inclined toward France, in the hope that Prussia would yield, and the telegrams give what was said against Prussia, but suppress everything against France. The press censorship was never more active and unscrupulous. In spite of its first wavering, the English press now, without exception, charges France with the responsibility for war. The Duc de Gramont's statement, with all its falsehoods, imposes on nobody. The interview between Benedetti and the King is perfectly understood as a premeditated insult by Benedetti, and a violation of every diplomatic usage, while Prussia's dignified attitude under repeated provocations has won her the sympathy of Europe.

BISMARCK.

The following extracts from a letter written by the New York *Tribune's* well-known correspondent, " G. W. S.," in 1866, entitled and describing " an Afternoon with Bismarck," will have renewed interest at the present time :

"The opinion we have in America that Bismarck is King of Prussia, and that the other is King only in name, is a wrong opinion. The royal authority is a very positive fact in this country, the ruling monarch, is a man of strong will, has a mind of his own on all public matters, and will not be led blindly about, nor submit himself readily to the guidance of any one. He requires to be persuaded, and will do no public act till he sees, or thinks he sees, it is in accordance with his own views. There is no country in Europe where the traditions of kingly rule are more potent, and no King who abides more firmly by his own convictions based upon hereditary opinions. In the Divine right and grace of God theories he believes profoundly. There was nothing from which he more shrunk than a war with Austria, which was to him the natural ally of Prussia and the representative of Imperialism in Europe. It was step by step that he advanced to the collision which his pride as a King and his judgment as a politician both told him was against his interests. But William is soldier as well as King, and when affairs came to such a crisis that he deemed his honor as an officer pledged to war, then, and then only, was war possible. It has been, one may suppose, not the easiest part of Count Bismarck's task for the last four years to conduct along his own path, which led inevitably, though not visibly, to war with Austria, such a man as King William.

"This notion of the King might be derived from the common talk in Berlin society as well as from Count Bismarck. In what follows I give not always the words, but always the substance of what Bismarck said, and much of its importance consists in the fact that he said it. The student of European politics will find several grave questions here answered positively, which heretofore have been answered only conjecturally. At the beginning he spoke with an air of great weariness, on which he himself commented, observing that he had been up for two nights, and that it was many months since he had had any rest. 'I am so tired,' said the Count, 'that if I could sleep for ten hours I should not wake, and if I were waked, I could sleep for ten more.' Upon this, which was said laughingly, I rose to go, but was put down in my chair again, and after a few sentences Count Bismarck began with a personal narrative. To those who are familiar with the history of the struggle in Prussia between Bismarck and the Liberals, and in Germany between Prussia and Austria, the bearing of this brief report will be sufficiently clear."

When the former Ministry resigned, in 1862, they had brought the King into collision with Parliament, and there left him. Count Bismarck, in assuming office, found himself obliged to continue this conflict. On the question of the army, the King and the Parliament could not be as one. The army needed a radical change in its organization, and having been mobilized in 1859, that opportunity had been taken as most convenient for the increase of the regiments. To-day every one sees that this step has proved essential to the success of Prussia, but its necessity was what no one would then believe, because the exigency of to-day was not foreseen, and its probable arrival could not be safely explained or predicted. But the regiments were increased, new officers were appointed, for whose pay there was no constitutional provision, and other large expenses were incurred. Parliament demanded that all this should be undone, but to disband the regiments and discharge the officers was impossible in view of such a future as has since arrived, nor could the money which had been paid out be recalled into the treasury. The budget, which Parliament demanded should be annulled, represented in fact, for the most part, sums of money already disbursed. The conflict was, therefore, not only irrepressible, but incapable of adjustment without abandoning a policy essential to the safety of Prussia, or without such explanations of that policy as would have insured in advance its defeat.

"In respect of foreign policy," said Count Bismarck, "I foresaw that the reorganized army was a necessity ; that upon it, and not upon Parliaments, or speeches before dinner, or after dinner, must Prussia depend for her hope of nationality. A nation she then was not, in the high sense of that word, nor was there hope that with her fantastical frontiers and outlying provinces her people should grow to think themselves one. The territorial configuration of the country was a source of weakness not to be obviated by even a far stronger sentiment of nationality than then existed, and it was before all things essential to the future of Germany that there should be first a Prussia able to insist on its opinions. I repeat, to declare such a policy in advance was to defeat it. The King would have opposed it utterly, Austria would have been forewarned and supplied with weapons, foreign courts would have scouted it as visionary, or have actively thwarted every step towards its accomplishment. To-day the work is done, but its final success I look upon as assured. North of the Main, Germany is one. * * * *

"The sudden and extraordinary success of Prussia alarmed the Emperor of the French in the prospect of a united Germany, a great German power established in a moment in the center of Europe and upon the frontier of France, *and his interposition in the peace negotiations was to prevent that complete union.* The part which he actually played was a part very different from that which he first contemplated. * * *. To have persisted at that moment would have been to go to war with France as well as with Austria.

"The result of the war is to make it possible that Prussia should be a nation capable to govern itself. She fought for defence, for own existence, and for Germany. Some people fancied it possible to unite Germany by speeches at Frankfort, but there were only two things which could make a Germany— a war or a revolution. Had Prussia not been able to lead the movement, she was likely to have been broken in pieces territorially, and Bavaria or Saxony would have had as much control in German politics as Prussia, while in European politics she might have been no better than another Belgium. The nationality of Prussia lay in her army. With the army as it was in 1859, it would have been impossible to fight. Two-thirds of her force was comprised in the Landwehr (the militia), unavailable for instant necessities, and the ranks were filled with men who had families and wished no war. It was necessary to break that up. I believe the Liberal party of Prussia now sees that a policy has been pursued during the last four years tending steadily to one end, and that the means employed were, if not the only, at least a sure method of reaching it. They clearly see that it was impossible to make such explanations as might have removed the necessity for the conflict I was obliged to carry on against them. I rejoice at their cordial acquiescence in the results that have been achieved, and that their assurance of good will and support are sincere I heartily believe—I should profoundly regret to doubt it—God forbid. On my part, be sure the feeling is cordial. The King's speech was sincere, and his desire to be on good terms with the Liberals is a genuine one, and I trust will continue. But

the influences which surround the King are well known and they cannot always be successfully opposed."

Much more was said about the King, which I must omit. The very interesting narrative which Count Bismarck gave of the circumstances attending his accession to office four years ago, and of his interviews with the King—these also must be passed over. I will only add that while the Minister President evidently finds his abilities often sorely tasked to persuade the King into his views of foreign and home policy, Count Bismarck, as a Prussian, is animated by a sentiment of loyalty perfectly genuine. He may speak of the King at times with some freedom, but he will always serve him faithfully. "You, as a Republican," said Count Bismarck, "cannot understand the feeling with which when called to the Ministry I proffered my services to the King. For four or five hundred years my ancestors had served his. That I should tell him when I thought him wrong, was not less necessary than that so long as I continued Minister I should obey. When it became impossible to obey, it was possible to resign." There is a contrast here which will not fail to suggest itself. On one side the Ministry, conducting the King step by step along a path he would not tread for one instant could he but see whither it led; on the other, the subject, professing and sincerely feeling the utmost loyalty to his sovereign. This is none the less human nature because it happens to be a contradiction. It is true also that loyalty to the Crown is a national sentiment among the Prussians, and that the throne of the Hohenzollerns stands firmer to-day than that of any royal house in Europe. I have heard from Liberals expressions of attachment to the King, *as* King, which would surprise those who are accustomed to think of Liberalism and Republicanism as one.

That Count Bismarck's opinions on constitutional government are not likely to find favor among those of us in America who believe in a government founded on ideas, I am very sure; but such as they are I give them. In respect to Prussian affairs, the question was considered in some details, but the general statement is at least compact and lucid. "In a government by written constitution there is no such thing as an absolute right on either side. A right absolute in terms must be subject to limitation in practice when its exercise comes in collision with another right equally perfect in theory, as must often be the case. Both are rights, but their co-enjoyment may prove quite impossible; then one must give way, and the welfare of the State must determine which. Be sure that in a parliamentary constitutional government, if you adopt the maxim *fiat justitia, pereat mundus,* it is the *pereat mundus* that will always come upon you."

The conversation touched briefly on American topics: "In our relations with the Uni-

MARSHAL MacMAHON.
Marſchall MacMahon.

ted States, I never had a doubt. The Tory party in Prussia, to which I am supposed to belong, at the outbreak of your war, besought the King to recognize the South. I opposed it inflexibly. To me it was clear that the North only could be the true ally of Prussia; with the South we had nothing in common. The Government of Prussia never wavered in its friendship for yours. [The sentence was uttered proudly, and the burning eyes flamed brighter than ever.] It is a traditional policy with us. Frederick the Great was, I think, the first European sovereign to recognize your independence. I am heartily glad to know that America understands and reciprocates the friendly feeling we have steadily maintained."

And here follows a curious statement—a fact not known to me before, and I think unpublished in America. "At the beginning of our war," said Count Bismarck, "Austria was stronger than we on the water, and Italy was not sure to us. It was proposed to me that the leading Southern naval officers should join us with 5,000 men and suitable vessels. They were not to come at all as the Confederate navy, but as individuals, and the most eminent officers among them were included in the offer. I consulted your Minister to know whether an acceptance of this offer would be offensive to the American Government. Mr. Wright was in doubt, and wrote to Washington. He received instructions to oppose the scheme, and I at once declined having anything to do with it. Semmes made the proposal."

ENTHUSIASTIC RECEPTION OF THE KING OF PRUSSIA AT BERLIN.

The King arrived at Berlin on the 16th of July from Ems, and found fully 100,000 people at the station waiting to escort him to the palace. The route lay through the splendid street, Unter den Linden, which was covered with flags and grandly illuminated for the occasion. All along the march the crowd shouted, cheered and sang national hymns. The King afterward repeatedly came forward and saluted the crowd from the palace windows.

The volunteering all over Prussia was extraordinary. The entire male population demanding arms.

The North German Parliament met on July 20th, to vote the necessary credits for war expenses.

King William sent to the Chamber of Commerce of Hamburg a grateful acknowledgment of the patriotic address of that body. He regrets the sacrifice which the honor of Germany exacts, but will do his duty, leaving the event in the hands of God.

On the night of the 17th of July, 1870, the first

INVASION OF PRUSSIANS UPON FRENCH SOIL

was made. They advanced as far as Sierck, in the Department of Moselle, for the evi-

dent purpose of destroying the railroad at that point; and on the same date, railway and telegraphic communication between France and Prussia was stopped. Count Benedetti arrived in Paris a few days before. Coming from Ems instead of Berlin, he did not receive his passport. He came to give the Emperor verbal explanations.

Baron Werther, the North German Minister, and all the members of his embassy left Paris the same day, for Berlin.

Before the departure of Baron Werther, the Secretary of State for Foreign Affairs, expressed his regret on account of the conduct of Prussia and the course Baron Werther himself had chosen to take before the final rupture of friendly relations. It is said that when the Baron returned here from Ems a few days ago, he neglected to call upon the Duke of Gramont until the latter had sent for him, and even then said "he had nothing to communicate." This coldness created great surprise.

Eight days before, the Count Bismarck sent by special messenger to Baron Werther, the Ambassador of the North German Confederation, an order to make no concession to the French Government. "Do not be too much impressed," Bismarck continues in his dispatch; "we are ready. Prolong the situation, if possible, to the 20th of July."

The French Journals argued from this, that Prussia meant war from the beginning, and only sought to gain time.

About this time, great activity prevailed in the Prussian Fortresses of Rastadt, in Baden. The soldiers of Baden, commanded by Prussian officers, were detailed to man the ramparts and parapets, and Prince Royal Frederick William took command of the armies of the States of Southern Germany.

On the 18th of July, the Emperor of the French left for the seat of war, with the Prince Imperial, a mere boy. "The Emperor, his father, wished it, and his mother, the Empress, did not object." Marshals MacMahon, Bazaine, and Canrobert, were appointed to command the main divisions of the Imperial French forces.

MARSHAL MACMAHON.

Marshal MacMahon, who held chief command of the French army, has well earned the reputation of a brave and skilful soldier. His father was a Lieutenant-General in the armies of France, and had him educated at the military school of St. Cyr. At the age of nineteen, he was sub-Lieutenant in the 4th Hussars. He exchanged into a regiment bound for Africa, where, on the hill of Monzai, Gen. Clanzel rewarded him with the Cross of the Legion of Honor, on account of the reckless daring he had displayed. An incident in the African campaign shows his intrepid character. At the close of the successful battle of Terchia, Gen. Achard wished to send an order to Col. Rulhieres at Blidah, between three and four miles off, to change the order of his march. This commission he entrusted to MacMahon, and offered him a squadron of mounted chasseurs as an escort. He declined their protection, and rode off alone. His journey lay entirely through the enemy's country, which was rugged and irregular. About six hundred yards from Blidah lay a ravine, broad, deep, and precipitous. MacMahon had risen close to the ravine, when suddenly he beheld a host of Arabs in full pursuit of him from every side. One look told him his chances. There was no alternative than to jump the treacherous abyss, or be butchered by his pursuers. He set his horse's head at the leap, put spur and whip to it, and cleared the ravine at a bound. The pursuing Arabs, dismayed, ventured no further, and only sent after the daring soldier a shower of bullets, as horse and rider rolled over on the other side, with the poor steed's leg broken. At the attack on Constantine he received further promotion. He continued connected with African warfare and public affairs until the opening of the Russian war, when more favorable opportunity to attain military fame presented itself. On the 8th of September, the perilous honor devolved on him of carrying the Malakoff, which formed the key of the defences of Sebastopol. The impetuous ardor of his troops proved irresistible. They entered the works, and maintained for hours a desperate conflict with the Russians. Pellissier, the Commander-in-Chief, believed the fort was mined. He sent MacMahon orders to retire. "I will hold my ground," was the reply, "dead or alive." Success crowned his bravery, and the tricolor soon floated above the fortress.

After more brilliant services in Algeria, the Austrian war next called him to the field. In one week from the commencement of hostilities, the French had driven back the Austrians across the Ticino, turned their flank, and forced them to give battle. With a suddenness which the French had not anticipated, the Austrians, on the 4th of June, 1859, with a force of 150,000 men, attacked the advancing French at the bridge of Magenta. The choicest French troops were there, and they met the attack with unbroken front, and drove back the foe with loss. But the Austrians, re-enforced at every moment, seemed destined to be the victors. MacMahon with the force under his command had, early in the day, crossed the river farther up to execute a flank movement. He heard the booming of the guns, and in a moment realized the situation. Hastily reversing his orders, he advanced against the enemy. The movement proved decisive. The Austrians were utterly routed, and fled in disorder, leaving 7,000 prisoners in the hands of the victors, and 20,000 soldiers killed and wounded on the field of battle. In 1861, MacMahon, now Duke of Magenta, attended the coronation of William of Prussia, whom now he encounters in deadly warfare. In physical appearance, Marshal MacMahon is rather below the middle size, with small, but well-shaped face and head, and spare, lightsome figure. He is now in his sixty-second year.

MARSHAL CANROBERT.

Marshal Canrobert has been the companion-in-arms of MacMahon on many a hard-fought field. At the age of twenty-six he left France for the African campaign, and took an active share in some desperate conflicts. In 1837, he received his first wound on the breach at the assault on Constantine. He fell at the side of Colonel Combes, who, dying, recommended him to Marshal Vallee, saying, "There is a brilliant future for this officer." Until 1849, Canrobert was engaged in the most desperate engagements of the Algerian campaigns, and on the accession of Prince Napoleon to power, he attached himself to his fortunes. He commanded the French forces in the Crimea for some time, and shared in all the earlier battles fought during the operations against Sebastopol. During the Italian war he displayed great daring at Magenta, and at Solferino was charged with duties upon which depended the issue of that battle.

THE EXCITEMENT IN PARIS.

The Empress arrived in Paris on the 17th of July, from St. Cloud, and was enthusiastically received.

A loan of six months treasury bonds, to the amount of 500,000,000 francs, was taken up in a few hours. The Credit Foncier and the Bank of France made efforts to monopolize the entire amount.

Passports were sent to the Count de Solms, in charge of the affairs of the Prussian Legation, the moment news was received that Prussian troops had crossed the frontier. Regiments were passing through the city all night on their way to the frontier. Great crowds gathered on the sidewalks, and cheered the soldiers as they passed. At all the gardens and places of amusement patriotic demonstrations were made.

The excitement was intense. No opposition to the war was made, and the press denounced the speech of M. Thiers in the CORPS LEGISLATIF.

It was announced that 280,000 French troops were ready to cross into Germany. The announcement that the Emperor intended to head the army in person, and by a series of rapid movements arrive at the Rhine before Prussia completed her defences, was received with great cheering.

An order was issued that the pupils of the second year at the MILITARY SCHOOL OF ST. CYR join the army, with the rank of sub-lieutenants.

PROCEEDINGS IN THE SENATE AND CORPS LEGISLATIF—DISCUSSION OF THE WAR QUESTION—THE DEMANDS OF THE GOVERNMENT ACCEDED TO.

In the Corps Législatif, M. Thiers, in a long speech, pronounced against the decla mation of the Government. He found, after all was said, that France had received satisfaction from Prussia, and war should not be made on her for a mere formality.

Prime Minister Ollivier responded to M. Thiers. He said it was impossible for the Government to do otherwise than it had done.

M. Thiers again took the floor. He recalled Mexico and Sadowa, and said the Government had made a new blunder.

The majority interrupted the speaker, but he continued amid the greatest agitation. When silence was restored, M. Gambetta demanded that all the correspondence had with Prussia be laid before the Corps Législatif.

Jules Favre seconded the motion in a long speech, asserting that France could not make war on the authority of telegraphic dispatches.

The Minister of Foreign Affairs replied that it was necessary to make war, and to do so immediately, in order to give Prussia no time to arm. If any other course was pursued he could no longer remain in the Ministry.

The question was then put to vote, and the demand for the correspondence was rejected by 164 against 84. The Corps then adjourned till 8 o'clock in the evening.

On reassembling, the following projects of law were brought forward:

First. To call the Garde Mobile into active service.

Second. To authorize the enlistment of volunteers for the war.

Third. To issue a demand loan of 50,000,-000 francs in aid of the army, and 16,000,000 in aid of the navy.

After a short debate, all these propositions were carried by the following vote: For, 246; against, 10. Many members of the party of the Left refused to vote.

In the Senate yesterday, after the Duke of Gramont had finished his declaration, M. Rouher asked if any Senator wished to speak. Loud cries of "no, no," followed.

M. Rouher then said: "As President of the Senate I will state that the Senate, responding for the nation, approves the conduct of the Government. We must place our hopes in Providence, and rely upon our courage for the triumph of our rights."

After the session the Senate proceeded in a body to St. Cloud, where they were received by the Emperor and Empress.

M. Rouher, President, said "the Senate thanked the Emperor for the permission of expressing to the Throne its patriotic sentiments. A monarchial combination, injurious to the prestige and security of France, had been mysteriously favored by Prussia. On our representations, Prince Leopold renounced the throne of Spain. Spain, who returns our friendship, then renounced a candidature so wounding to us. Without doubt, immediate danger was thus avoided; but our legitimate complaint remains. Was it not evident that a foreign power, to prejudice our honor and interests, wished to disturb the balance of power in Europe? Had we not the right to demand of that power guarantees against a possible recurrence of such an attempt? This is refused, and the dignity of France insulted. Your Majesty draws the sword, and the country is with you, eager for and proud of the occasion. You have waited long; but during this time you raised to perfection the military organization of France. By your care France is prepared. Her enthusiasm proves that, like your Majesty, she will not tolerate wrong. Let our august Empress become again the depositary of the imperial power. The great bodies of the State surround Her Majesty with their absolute devotion. The nation has faith in her wisdom and energy. Let your Majesty resume with noble confidence the command of the legions you led at Magenta and Solferino. If peril has come, the hour of victory is near, and soon a grateful country will decree to her children the honors of triumph; soon Germany will be freed from the domination which has oppressed her, and peace will be restored to Europe through the glory of our arms. Your Majesty, who so recently received a proof of the national good will, may then once more devote yourself to reforms, the realization of which is only retarded. Time only is needed to conquer."

The Emperor warmly thanked the President and members of the Senate.

The war feeling had, by this time, taken entire control of the inhabitants of Paris.

The Duke of Gramont, after leaving the Senate Chamber, was greeted by crowds upon the streets with most enthusiastic cheers and plaudits.

A demonstration was made in front of the residence of M. Thiers to express dissatisfaction at his course in the Corps Législatif. This was followed by a demonstration in his favor. The latter, the *Journal de France* says, was not respectably supported, and was the work of "unknown creatures."

The troops in Paris sang the "Marseillaise," and the artistes at the various places of amusement were allowed to sing it also, the audiences in all cases joining enthusiastically. Everywhere the boulevards and streets were crowded with people almost wild with excitement.

A FORMAL DECLARATION OF WAR FROM FRANCE TO PRUSSIA.

On the 18th of July, 1870. a formal declaration of war was sent by France to Berlin. France also informed Prussia that she will not use explosive bullets if Prussia will not.

THE FORMAL DECLARATION.

THE EXCUSE OF FRANCE—IMMENSE PREPARATIONS—POPULAR DEMONSTRATIONS ON BOTH SIDES.

An extra edition of the *Constitutionnel*, issued at noon, announced that in consequence of the insult offered to Benedetti (the French Minister), France accepts the war which Prussia offers.

The French declaration of war is based on the following causes:

First : The insult offered at Ems to Count Benedetti, the French Minister, and its approval by the Prussian Government.

Second : The refusal of the King of Prussia to compel the withdrawal of Prince Leopold's name as a candidate for the Spanish throne.

Third : The fact that the King persisted in giving the Prince liberty to accept the crown.

The declaration concludes as follows:

"The extraordinary constitutional changes in Prussia awaken the slumbering recollections of 1814. Let us cross the Rhine, and avenge the insults of Prussia. The victors of Jena survive."

The Bundesrath of the North German Confederation met in Berlin. The Prussian Diet was already in session. The chiefs of all parties assured the King of their unqualified approval of his dignified and energetic attitude.

The belligerents engaged to respect the neutrality of Belgium, yet troops were rapidly concentrating at Antwerp and other strategic points. The specie and bullion in the National Bank at Antwerp were removed to the citadel, and an issue of paper money announced.

THE UNITED STATES.

German mass meetings were held throughout the Union. These led to the organization of Aid Societies, etc., etc.

THE MASS MEETING AT STEINWAY HALL, NEW YORK CITY.

(By our own Correspondent.)

New York City, July 21st, 1870.

The war enthusiasm prevailing among the German population of this city culminated last night in a grand mass meeting at Steinway Hall, called by a Committee of the leading Germans residing in this city. At 8 o'clock, the appointed time of the meeting, the hall was full to repletion. Not only the 4,000 seats, but every inch of standing-room in balcony and aisles, was occupied, and crowds overflowed into the halls, about every door-way, vainly striving for admission. Notwithstanding the crowd, and the enthusiasm which prevailed, the whole proceeding was notable for the orderly and decorous conduct characteristic with the German people on such occasions. They came and went unmolested, " paceable as kin be." As the policeman expressed it, " they're all on the won side!" Nothing like a disturbance occurred to mar the demonstration.

In the Hall, the stage was appropriately decorated with American and German flags; the invited guests seated in rows along the rear and sides of the stage, and the band in the orchestra chairs; the space in front, about the speakers' stand, being left open.

Beside the speakers of the evening, whose names are given below, there were many prominent citizens among the 50 gentlemen seated upon the stage, including Mr. Petrarch, the Secretary of the Society for the Aid of the Wounded and Sick Soldiers of Prussia, and of Soldiers' Widows; and Gen. Sigel and Messrs. Wm. Steinway, E. Tauer, President of the New German American Bank, Hugo Wesendouck, Dr. Krakowitzer, and Messrs. Bauendahl, Schlesinger, Roelker, Kunoth, and other well-known merchants.

A feature of the evening was the singing of the Liederkranz and Arion Societies, who joined forces for the occasion. At about 8:15 they filed across Union-square, arm in arm, numbering about 100 voices, and entered the rear door of the hall. "Die Macht am Rhein" and "Was ist des Deutschen Vaterland" were received with great applause. The appropriate words of the latter, the magnificent national air of the whole German-speaking race, aroused tremendous enthusiasm. The very first lines embody the feeling which binds all the American Germans together as a unit against France:

> " Was ist des Deutschen Vaterland?
> Ist's Preussenland? Ist's Schwabenland?
> Ist's wo am Rhein die Rebe glueht?
> Ist's wo am Belt die Moewe zieht?
> O nein, nein, nein,
> Sein Vaterland muss groesser sein.
>
> *   *   *   *   *   *
>
> " Was ist des Deutschen Vaterland?
> So nenne endlich mir das Land !
> So weit die deutsche Zunge klingt
> Und Gott im Himmel Lieder singt—
> Das soll es sein,
> Das ganze Deutschland soll es sein."

A work of art was exhibited during the evening, which caused much amusement. It was a brilliantly-colored banner, representing the "End of the War." The short and somewhat pursy figure of Napoleon was represented as hanging by the neck, his characteristic countenance distorted with anguish, while beneath the figure of Peace waves the banner of victorious Prussia before the eyes of a returned soldier, and other characters.

The business of the meeting was commenced by Mr. Petrarch, who called the assembly to order at 8 o'clock. He nominated ex-Gov. Salomon for Chairman, who was chosen by acclamation.

SPEECH OF EX-GOVERNOR SALOMON.

Gov. Salomon then spoke as follows :

FELLOW GERMAN BROTHERS :—In the first place, I thank you for the honor you confer upon me by making me Chairman of this mass meeting. Among the first remembrances of us German Americans is the storm through which this country passed, and in which we showed our loyalty. When this country, in her hour of need, called you, you responded, and your blood, spilled on the battle-field and recorded in history, shows that Germans know how to fight for their land of adoption. Therefore we dare say that this meeting, where we expect to express our sympathy for our mother country, and stand by it as much as our duty to the laws of our adopted country permit, is not amiss ; America is our father, and Germany our mother. We owe allegiance to both. The man who in 1848 could cause women and children to be killed in the streets of Paris, who ever since has kept Europe in a continued fear; he, with one foot in the grave, tries to preserve his tottering throne for his son, and has declared war upon Germany to give the mercurial and vain-glorious Frenchman something to think of beside revolution. The reason he gave for the war has been taken away—the German Prince who was to ascend the throne of Spain has withdrawn. But Napoleon feels his throne giving way. The farce of the Plebiscitum did not help him. He wishes to maintain his power at the expense of German blood and German unity.

The French jealousy of German power is the true cause of the present conflict. Germany must be divided, annihilated, to make France greater, and therefore we stand on the eve of one of the most tremendous wars ever witnessed, and which will decide the fate of Germany. Germany should be united in taking up the glove thrown down by France. France wants to see Germany divided, and therefore it wishes war. Let us be united. We Germans of America should send to our brothers in fatherland the tiding that we are with them in the fight and have brotherly feelings with them; that we will do all we can for them, without forgetting our duty to the United States. Once more I say, let us be united.

THE RESOLUTIONS.

Ex-Governor Salomon continued: "Mr. Petrarch will now read to you resolutions which we propose for your adoption." The resolutions were then read, and are as follows:

Common sense demands that international relations be governed by the interests of nations and not by those of princes. Every nation has the right to determine its own destiny, and no other people is authorized to cripple it. If Germany is weary of its internal discords of many centuries, and if the one nation desires a consolidation under one government, no right of veto is given to any power on earth. If France covets the leadership in Europe, Germany is not, therefore, bound to do it the favor to remain in weakness. If France chooses an emperor, and if the throne of this emperor is on a firm foundation but so long as he is the mightiest of princes, this does not bind the German people to lay the insignia of their inalienable sovereignty at the feet of the Gallican Cæsar. Not against Prussia, but against strengthened Germany his ire is directed. To Germany he has thrown down the gauntlet to mortal combat. Therefore not Prussia alone, but the entire German nation rises in its full majesty against the audacious man, who presumes to trample nations in the dust to gratify his princely lust. The Germans of

America have become citizens of another country, but they have not divested themselves of their nationality. The national cause is their cause. Unanimously they stand by it, firmly resolved to do all in their power, not inconsistent with their duties as American citizens, to turn the war which has been commenced by France, without any just cause whatever, to a triumph for Germany. It is therefore

Resolved, 1. That we herewith organize a society for the purpose of furthering the cause of Germany, and more particularly for the purpose of nursing wounded German soldiers and of assisting in the support of the surviving widows and orphans.

2. That an Executive Committee, consisting of Philip Bissinger, Dr. H. von Holst, F. Kilian, Dr. E. Krakowitzer, Henry Merz, Oswald Ottendorfer, Theo. F. C. Petrarch, Edward Salomon, Emil Sauer, Prof. A. J. Schem, Gen. Franz Sigel, William Steinway, L. J. Stiastny, and Hugo Wesendonck, be intrusted with the management of all affairs of this society.

3. That every German society of the city of New York and vicinity be invited to send one delegate to the General Committee, whose duty it shall be to make proper arrangements for the collection of contributions of money, clothing, linen, lint, etc., during the continuance of the war.

4. That both the Executive and the General Committee be authorized to increase their respective numbers as they may deem proper, and to enter into communication with similar societies of other cities and towns.

In accordance with the principles above enunciated, it is further

Resolved, That humanity and modern civilization demand that the inviolability of private persons and private property be recognized by belligerent powers also at sea; that the exertions of the United States and of other powers to embody this principle in the law of nations, deserve the highest regard; and that, considering that this principle was first brought to recognition by the United States in their treaty with Frederick the Great in the year 1785, was subsequently, after various other efforts, brought to the attention of the powers of Europe by the well-known amendment proposed by Mr. Marcy to the Treaty of Paris of 1856, and has thereby obtained in history the name of the "American Amendment;" considering further, that this principle has already heretofore been recognized by all the great Powers of Europe, with the exception of England, that particularly Napoleon I. and also the present Emperor of France have given their unconditional adherence to its righteousness, and that the King of Prussia has even, in case of reciprocity, elevated it in the year 1866 to a permanent law, we deem this the proper time of the Government of the United States to use at once all peaceful means at their command to secure the adherence also of France to this principle, and its respect by the belligerents during the present war, and also, as soon as possible, its recognition by all civilized nations, for all future time, as a principle of international law.

Resolved further, That, to this and this meeting do appoint a Committee, consisting of Edward Salomon, Joseph Seligman, and Oswald Ottendorfer, whose duty it shall be to lay the foregoing resolution before the President of the United States and the Secretary of State, and generally to take such action as they may deem proper to obtain from the Government a fulfilment of its great traditional duty to humanity.

SPEECH OF SENATOR CARL SCHURZ.

The resolutions were unanimously adopted amid loud cheers, and after singing of "*Die Wacht am Rhein*" by the "Arion and Liederkrantz Singers' Union," Governor Salomon introduced General Carl Schurz, who was received with thunders of applause. He said:

MY GERMAN FELLOW-CITIZENS: I come to you to-night exhausted by long work and a prolonged session of the United States Congress. I don't know whether I shall be able to speak to you as I might have wished. I had hoped to have some rest, when the call came which will give no rest to any one. I wish to mingle my voice with the voice of the mass meeting which gives expression not only to the feeling of Germans, but of Americans as well. In this moment the whole of America speaks. A bloody war tragedy develops itself on the Eastern Continent. We all know that war is the worst of evils, and he who begins it without sufficient reason takes upon himself a terrible responsibility. Spain tried to have a German Prince ascend a weak and worthless throne. France considered the choice of that German Prince an insult. Could any one with clear common sense imagine that in this, the nineteenth century, the century of civilization, a war of succession could revolutionize Europe?— Kings may be relatives; they should not forget that nations are related also.

The first ground upon which war was declared was a lie. The Prince had withdrawn before it was declared. The second point was the insult of the King to a French Ambassador. Why was this insult offered? Because he did what no gentleman should do or does. He wished, while the King was drinking mineral waters, to put him to an ultimatum, and he was rightly reprimanded. Kings, as a general thing, are not favorites in this country, but William has acted as a gentleman. [Loud cheers.] Every German should be glad that a man is on the throne of Prussia who dares show his teeth, and is not intimidated by bravado.

Now, this so-called insult was only another subterfuge. Ask Napoleon if he would have acted as Benedetti did, or if having done so, he would have considered the consequence as an insult? No one is deceived by words, and

no one believes the pretext. Every one knows that France wishes to dictate. Napoleon well knows that French honor is a peculiar honor. When any nation acquires one foot of ground, France wants the same, or considers the aggrandizement as an insult. When taking a province herself, she does not wish to have anything said. The policy of Napoleon has been to consolidate the Roman nationality, at the same time he tried to upset German union. At the head of France, Napoleon considers every concentration of power and union in Germany as a personal insult to France, because it lessens its prestige. Balance of power in Europe means, according to Napoleon, that France shall be a little heavier than the rest. And now the two great Powers of Europe stand armed in opposition. The war will be one of unprecedented extent, and will decide the future fate of Germany, maybe of Europe.

In one of the evening papers the story of an Englishman is given, who, having seen the two armies in position, says: "In the French camp there is loud and hilarious enthusiasm. The soldiers are drinking, shouting, and cheering. In the German camp all is quiet, but that quiet bespeaks determination." And it is a good sketch. With the usual French enthusiasm and bravado, the French army will cross the Rhine and enter Germany, there to be silently, but firmly, met by German bayonets. The Germans no longer are the soldiers of Jena, as Napoleon vainly tries to make his army believe. They have learned since then, and Sadowa shows what they have learned. But what will be the end of this all? Not evil only. One great thing has already been accomplished.

Germany is united. It was not so a week ago. The factions still rankled and glowed in the German breast. To-day nothing is there but a brotherly feeling, a sentiment of hate against an aggressive tyrant. Naturally our hopes are with our flag. The victory of Prussia will be the fall of despotism; the fall of a system which has made slaves of Europeans; the fall of a system which has spread damnable poverty and ignominy, and above all, it will be the erection of a great kingdom in the centre of Europe, a kingdom which will be peace in reality and not in word only.

Therefore, it is not strange that the Germans and Americans are with us. A finer instinct makes the American see the finer and truer nature of the German. He knows that the day is not far distant when balance of power in Europe will be a name only. He knows that in case of need he can safely rely on German arms. It has not forgotten our help in the late struggle. Therefore, America is on the German side. Is it not right—nay, is it not a duty that we all should help? I do call on you as German born. He who could forget father or mother, cannot be a good citizen. Let us not fear that America will mistake or misconstrue our action. We could not love our new country, our land of

PRIME MINISTER OLLIVIER.

Premierminifter Emile Ollivier.

GEN. ACHILLE FAILLY.

General Achille Failly.

adoption, if we did forget our old country, the land of our birth.

Let us help and act at the same time in accordance with the laws here. These laws do not forbid our sympathy, nor do they forbid us to help the sick and wounded. Let us then be united and give what we can, and let us daily send to our brothers over the water the message: "Fight for Fatherland. The Germans of the whole world are with you."

After several speeches from well-known gentlemen, the audience dispersed with loud cries of "*vive la Prussia!*"

WHY THE PEOPLE OF AMERICA SYMPATHIZE WITH PRUSSIA.

While the French Emperor was doing all in his power to injure and humiliate the United states during the great war of the Rebellion, there were two hundred thousand German-born citizens fighting under the flag of the Union, and offering their lives for the liberties of America. These two facts, in themselves, go far to explain the sympathies of the American people with Germany in the present war.

Many things are said and performed under the excitement of the moment by our German-American citizens, and afterward repented of.

It was at least in bad taste to display a picture of the French Emperor suspended from a gibbet, at a meeting participated in by an American Senator, an American ex-General, and an American ex-Governor. The American people are not at war with the French Emperor. Our more excitable citizens of German birth must not make any mistakes which will injure their own cause in America.

The French Emperor should not meddle with other people's business. He interfered in Mexican affairs, and lost by it. He meddled with American affairs to help Jeff. Davis, and suffered by it. He was humiliated in his attempts at interfering with German affairs four years ago. In now meddling with Spanish and Prussian affairs, he may meet with the same kind of bad luck which he has previously suffered by this officious intermeddling.

The war is not between France and Prussia. Neither is it between Napoleon and King William. It is a war between the people of Prussia and the Napoleonic dynasty, for the integrity of the Prussian nationality. In Prussia, the king counts for very little. He is old; is soon to pass away, and to be succeeded by a liberal heir. He is now, absolutist and believer in his own divine right as he is, merely the representative of the demands of the German people for a complete nationality, and of the instinctive resentment which all Germans, whether Prussians, Bavarians, citizens of the smaller German states, or even Austrians, feel against the French aggression. Napoleon, on the other hand, is in no sense a representative of the French people. By skilful manipulations he may succeed in arousing popular pride and stimulating national resentments to such a pitch that France may ultimately support him; but in the outset he was merely the persistent gambler he has always been—driven, however, into sore straits—and is playing, in a desperate emergency, his last card. Whatever else may happen, it is impossible that the American people can sympathize with him. If the question were between him and King William, they would sympathize with neither. As it is, cherishing no ill-will to the French, and earnestly wishing them the deliverance which is likely to come from the present complications, the Americans, nevertheless, are likely to give the sympathies of their whole hearts to the cause of the Prussian people, with which is bound up so much of hope, progress, and the possibility of freedom and national growth, not merely for Prussia, but even for the true France of the future.

It is given to man as his chiefest blessing to hope against hope, and we do not despair of the final deliverance of all nations from kingcraft. But we are warned by the results of all recent struggles not to expect it in our day. The Polish and Hungarian rebellions, the reconstruction of Italy and the last Spanish revolution, as well as the submission of France and Prussia to imperialism, are sufficient to prove that emancipation of the masses is yet far distant. Remembrance of these things ought to diminish the universal amazement that there is a war of succession in our time.

ACTUAL OPERATIONS COMMENCED.

About the 17th of July, 1870, skirmishing commenced between the advance guards along the frontier. Four killed and seven wounded on the Prussian side. The French loss was double these numbers.

PROCLAMATION FROM NAPOLEON.

Paris, July 23d, 1870.

FRENCHMEN: There are in the life of a people solemn moments when the national honor, violently excited, presses itself irresistibly, rises above all other interests, and applies itself with the single purpose of directing the destinies of the nation. One of those decisive hours has now arrived for France. Prussia, to whom we have given evidence during and since the war of 1856, of the most conciliatory disposition, has held our good will of no account, and has returned our forbearance by encroachments. She has aroused distrust in all quarters necessitating exaggerated armaments, and has made of Europe a camp where reign disquiet and fear of the morrow. A final incident has disclosed the instability of the international understanding, and shown the gravity of the situation. In the presence of her new pretensions Prussia was made to understand our claims. They were evaded and followed with contemptuous treatment. Our country manifested profound displeasure at this action, and quickly a war cry resounded from one end of France to the other.

There remains for us nothing but to confide our destinies to the chance of arms. We do not make war upon Germany, whose independence we respect. We pledge ourselves that the people composing the great Germanic nationality shall dispose freely of their destinies. As for us, we demand the establishment of a state of things guaranteeing our security and assuring the future. We wish to conquer a durable peace, based on the true interests of the people, and to assist in abolishing that precarious condition of things when all nations are forced to employ their resources in arming against each other.

The glorious flag of France, which we once more unfurl in the face of our challengers, is the same which has borne over Europe the civilizing ideas of our great revolution. It represents the same principles; it will inspire the same devotion.

FRENCHMEN: I go to place myself at the head of that gallant army, which is animated by love of country and devotion to duty. That army knows its worth, for it has seen victory follow its footsteps in the four quarters of the globe. I take with me my son. Despite his tender years he knows the duty his name imposes upon him, and he is proud to bear his part in the dangers of those who fight for our country. May God bless our efforts. A great people defending a just cause is invincible.

NAPOLEON.

IMPEACHMENT OF NAPOLEON III.

The Paris *Soir* publishes from the pen of M. Edmond About, the following masterly review of Napoleon's official career, and statement of the sufferings he has entailed upon France:

May I be mistaken! But it seems to me that we are now beginning to pay very dearly our collective abdication in 1851 and 1852. A people may imagine itself in clover when it has relieved itself from the trouble of managing its own affairs, and when it has confided its destinies to the hands of a bold and able man. The Constitution leaves to this man the power of commanding the land and sea forces, declaring war and making treaties of peace and alliance. What an excellent pretext for humble individuals to spare themselves the trouble of thinking about public matters, and laying themselves out to make as much money as possible in their own private occupations. But let us suppose that the master elected by the people has more imagination than genius; that he has the appetite of a conqueror without the firmness and the settled purpose necessary to success; that he reckons too much upon his star, and expects from luck and the mistakes of others the results which he ought deliberately to prepare for himself. Let us suppose that he lives from hand to mouth, tempting fortune instead of making himself master of it. Always advancing, drawing back, and oscillating between the possible and the impossible, and what is more serious, between the just and the unjust; now a champion of Right, and to-morrow a champion of State necessity; a Revolutionist or a Reactionist, just as it may happen, and ever ready to make a hash of his principles for the sake of expediency, it is not at all impossible that one fine day 38,000,000 of men may rouse themselves, and express their dissatisfaction in a way not easily to be dealt with. Frenchmen, my good friends, only think of the great things which you have done by procuration within the last twenty years. On your behalf your governors have dreamed for you the conquest of the world, and universal monarchy, or at least the supremacy of Europe, with the extension of your frontiers. In 1849, when you were nominally Republicans, you violently put down the Roman Republic; you fought in Italy for that Divine right which you have suppressed in Paris: you restored the Pope, who does not thank you, and pays you with all sorts of affronts. At Sebastopol you humiliated but did not weaken Russia: *you sacrificed a hundred thousand men and spent a million of money, with no other result than to draw down upon you the hatred and rancor of a powerful nation.* It is true that Turkey owes you a debt of gratitude for having postponed the solution of the great Eastern problem; but wretched Turkey would be of no use to you in case of war. In Lombardy you weakened Austria, aggrandized Victor Emmanuel, and favored the fusion of small, harmless States with a great Power. And now you have been clever enough to alienate that Power which owes everything to you by keeping it out of its capital. After having grouped a real nation around the small King of Sardinia, you have forced that Règalantuomo to be your enemy. You have sought adventures in China and Mexico. The great American Republic was from its beginning the friend and ally of France. You constrained it to forget that it owed its existence to you. In the war of the Secession, when you should have sympathized with the cause of the North, you shut your ear to true principles. Your interests, as you understood them, led you to side with the South, but you had not the courage or the sincerity to act upon your opinion. You only gave to the Slavery party a hesitating and sterile support. *The Union was restored in spite of you, and its first movement was to make you evacuate Mexico.* In Germany you tried surreptitiously to weaken Austria by Prussia, and Prussia by Austria. Your diplomatists, who are supposed to be the pick and choice of human ability, warranted success. After a long and ruinous war the Austrians, your secret allies, who you had calculated, would be the victors, were beaten, and the Prussians, your enemies, became masters of Germany Prussia allied herself with Italy, and your only compensation is the alliance of Austria, who, thanks to you, is reduced to the last degree of impotency. Such, my dear French people, is the result of your campaigns and your negotiations. Peace and war have been almost equally fatal to you. And you may be very sure that, on the first opportunity, Prussia, Russia, America, and Italy will be ready to combine to pay off old scores. This election of a King of Spain may be as good an excuse as any other.

SAARBRUCK.

THE ENGAGEMENT, JULY 31ST, 1870.

The engagement at Saarbruck, on Sunday, July 31st, was between a small detachment forming a Prussian outpost and three divisions of French infantry supporting 23 guns. The affair was of slight importance, and the loss trifling on each side.

In spite of the apparent importance of maintaining railway connection at Saarbruck, the Prussians never seriously prepared to defend it, and their movements were independent of the Saarbruck line. Considerable bodies of troops entered Saarbruck at different times, but not as a garrison. The town itself is indefensible, unless the heights on the French side are occupied by a large force. In fact, those heights were only picketed by Prussians.

The attack repulsed on Saturday, July30th, was a sufficient warning of the French intentions, but the Prussians took no further steps, even when the French subsequently occupied the woods.

The Emperor, on his return to Metz after the battle, sent the following telegraphic dispatch to the Empress :

"Louis has received his baptism of fire. He was admirably cool, and little impressed. A division of Frossard's command carried the heights overlooking the Saar. The Prussians made a brief resistance. Louis and I were in front where the bullets fell about us. Louis keeps a ball he picked up. The soldiers wept at his tranquillity. We lost an officer and ten men. NAPOLEON."

"Received his baptism of fire" and "the soldiers wept at his tranquillity," are lines too good to be omitted in history, and will be laughed at in after years as they are at this time. The idea of a man like Napoleon III, who placed himself upon the throne of France, first by promises of holding the freedom of that country at heart, and then held himself there by the aid of cut-throats ; and such a man asking God to aid him in maintaining a cruel war against an upright and peace-loving people. This was the man who, standing in need of a target for his soldiers, ordered them to fire upon some of the peasantry who were passing at the time, and actually killed forty harmless men, women and children by his fiendish command.

But how pleasant it is to turn from this cruel monarch, and contemplate the quiet and noble behavior of that man who has always thought of his God and people. Let the impartial read King William's proclamation, and they cannot but agree that further praise of that noble man is unnecessary :

"All Germany stands united against a neighboring State which has surprised us by declaring war without justification. The safety of the Fatherland is threatened. Our honor and our hearths are at stake. To-day I assume command of the whole army. I advance cheerfully to a contest which in former times our fathers, under similar circumstances, fought gloriously. The whole Fatherland and myself trust confidently in you. The Lord God will be with our righteous cause."

The affair at Saarbruck was regarded as wholly unimportant. The Prussians at no time contemplated holding that town in force.

The Emperor wished to gain possession of Saarbruck, because it commands the valley of the Saar and the railway to Treves ; and as the town proved of no material advantage, the French were allowed to take it without any stout resistance being made. They afterwards found themselves in a position similar to the man who won the elephant in a lottery—"they could not *keep it.*"

Following close upon this battle came the more important one of

WEISSENBURG.

On Friday, August 5th, an official account of this battle was received at Berlin, dated Thursday, 4th :

"We have won a brilliant but bloody victory. The left wing was the attacking body, and consisted of the Fifth and Eleventh Prussian Corps, with the Second (Bavarian). This force carried by an assault, under the eyes of the Prince Royal, the fortress of Weissenburg and the heights between Weissenburg and Geisburg.

"Douay's division of Marshal MacMahon's corps was splendidly defeated, being driven from its camp. Gen. Douay himself was killed. Five hundred prisoners were taken. None of them were wounded. Many Turcos were among the captured. The Prussian Gen. Kirchback was slightly wounded. The Royal Grenadiers and the 50th Regiment of the line suffered heavy losses."

THE BATTLE OF WEISSENBURG.

"The French infantry in action at Weissenburg and Geisburg belonged to the 1st Corps ; the cavalry to the 5th Corps. Except an attack undertaken to cover the retreat, the French stood on the defensive during the whole engagement. Most of the French troops in the engagement conducted themselves with much spirit, and held their ground manfully. Only after retreat had become inevitable did they appear as if seized by a sudden panic. At this crisis troops of the Corps MacMahon, which had not yet been under fire, threw away their caps, knapsacks, tents, etc., and decamped, leaving even their provisions behind them. The Algerian troops exhibited the same temper as the French. There was no perceptible difference between them and their European comrades.

"The infantry, whose battalions were not above 800 strong, opened fire at 1500 paces. This makes hitting a mere matter of chance, and has a tendency to demoralize a man in the use of his weapon. Our practice of forming company columns and outflanking the enemy's tirailleurs fully answered. The French cavalry, even if numerically equal to our own, invariably declined attack. Our artillery fired slower, but much more effectively, than the French. The mitrailleuse battery fired three rounds at a distance of 1800 paces against our artillery, but did no damage. It was soon silenced by our guns."

"I am now about to relate an incident," writes a friend of mine, from the battle field, "which will make a draft even upon your faith, Professor; and that is, that one portion of our line retained all that day a position within about fifteen yards of the enemy's works. I am proud to say that I belonged to the brigade who so gallantly accomplished this feat. Col. Yawn commanded in person, and the conduct of our eight hundred (for of that number our brigade consisted) deserves mention; and we claim, with an excusable conceit, that it was as splendid a stroke of heroism as ever lit up the story of 'The glory we call Greece, and the grandeur we call Rome.' Through the live-long day our men held their line, within fifteen yards of the enemy, and all his force could not dislodge us. Repeatedly during the day the French formed double columns of attack, to come over the walls and assail us; and the officers could be heard encouraging their troops by telling them 'that there are only two or three hundred of them.' But the moment the Frenchmen showed themselves above the parapets, a line of fire was opened on them from 'our eight hundred,' and many a 'Frenchy' fell prone under our swift avenging bullets.

"The sequel to this bit of history is as curious as the deed itself—for while the French dared not venture out to assail Col. Yawn's men, neither could *he*, nor his *command*, recede from their perilous position. He could not get back to us, and it seemed impossible for us to reach him. In this dilemma the ingenious device was hit upon of running a 'sap,' or ziz-zag trench, up from our line to his. In this way a working party were able to dig their way up to where they lay, begrimed with powder, and worn down with fatigue. They were thus rescued from a situation at once disagreeable and dangerous. But Yawn, our gallant leader, he came not away alive. Since eleven o'clock in the morning he had lain behind the bulwarks his valor defended—*a corpse*. There were other scenes along those lines drawn so close up to the enemy equally as grave, but I'll venture to say that not one of our eight hundred but would gladly have

changed places with our noble leader, if in his dying moments he could have known that Colonel Yawn, the gallant and brave Yawn! was still among the living."

Lay him down, for he is sleeping; fold his blanket o'er his breast,
In death's cold and silent slumber, let the soldier calmly rest;
Wave our banner far above him, 'twas for it he nobly died,
And 'tis well that ye should plant it, proudly waving by his side.

'Twas for us he left his kindred, for our homes he fought and fell,
And endured toils, hardships, sickness, that no one but him could tell;
Now he rests, and all is over, and his spirit dwells above,
Far above the din of battle, with our country's God he loved.

And so ends my friend's letter. I know not whether the verses given are original with him, or whether he quotes at random, but to my idea they are very pretty, and let that be my excuse for placing them before the kind reader.

And now we have the

BATTLE OF WOERTH.

"On the 5th of August reliable intelligence was received at the headquarters of the 3d Army that Marshal MacMahon was busily engaged in concentrating his troops on the hills west of Woerth, and that he was being reinforced by constant arrivals by railway. In consequence of these advices, it was resolved to lose no time in effecting a change of front, which had been determined upon a few days previously, but not yet executed. The 2d Bavarian and the 5th Prussian Corps were to remain in their respective positions at Lembach and Prenschdorf; the 11th Prussian Corps was to wheel to the right and encamp at Holschloch, with van pushed forward towards the river Sauer; and the 1st Prussian Corps was to advance into the neighborhood of Lobsann and Lampertsloch. The cavalry division remained at Schonenburg, fronting west. The Corps Werder (Wurtemburg and Baden divisions) marched to Reimerswiller, with patrols facing the Haguenau forest.

"The 5th Prussian Corps, on the evening of the 5th, pushed its van from its bivouac at Prenschdorf on to the height east of Woerth. On the other side of the Sauer, numerous camp fires of the enemy were visible during the night, the French outposts occupying the heights west of the Sauer, opposite Woerth and Gunstett. At dawn of the 6th, skirmishes commenced along the line of the outposts, which caused the Prussian vanguard to send a battalion into Woerth. At 8 o'clock steady firing was heard on the right (Bavarian) flank. This and the fire the enemy directed against Woerth caused us to station the entire artillery of the 5th Prussian Corps on the heights east of this place and try to relieve the Bavarians. A little later the 5th Corps was ordered to break off the engagement, it being the intention of our generals to begin the battle against the concentrated forces of the enemy only when the change of front had been effected and the entire German army was ready to be brought into action. At 7.45 o'clock the 4th Division (Bothmer) of the 2d Bavarian Corps (Hartmann), induced by the heavy fire of the outposts near Woerth, had left their bivouac at Lembach, and, proceeding by Mattstall and Langen-Salzbach, after a sharp engagement penetrated as far as Neschwiller, where they spread, fronting to the south. At 10½ this Bavarian Corps, supposing the order to break off the engagement which had been given to the 5th Prussians to extend to themselves, withdrew to Langen-Salzbach. The enemy, being thus no longer pressed on his left, turned all his strength with the greatest energy against the 5th Prussians at Woerth. Reinforcements were continually thrown in by rail. Finding the enemy in earnest on this point, and perceiving the 11th Prussians to approach vigorously in the direction of Gunstett, the 5th Prussians immediately proceeded to the attack, so as to defeat the enemy if possible before he had time to concentrate. The 20th Brigade was the first to defile through Woerth, and marched towards Elsasshausen and Froschwiller; it was promptly followed by the 19th Brigade. The French stood their ground with the utmost pertinacity, and their fire was crushing. Whatever the gallantry of our 10th Division, it did not succeed in overcoming the obstinate resistance of the enemy, Eventually, the 9th Division being drawn into the fight, the whole 5th Corps found itself involved in the sanguinary conflict raging along the heights west of Woerth.

"At 1¼ P. M., orders were given to the 1st Bavarian Corps (Von der Tann) to leave one of its two divisions where it stood, and, sending on the other as quick as possible by Lobsann and Lampertsloch, seize upon the enemy's front in the gap between the 2d Bavarian Corps at Langen-Salzbach and the 5th Prussian Corps at Woerth. The 11th Prussians were ordered to advance to Elsasshausen, skirt the forest of Niederwald, and operate against Froschwiller. The Wurtemburg Division was to proceed to Gunstett, and follow the 11th Prussians across the Sauer; the Baden Division was to remain at Sauerburg.

"At 2 o'clock the combat had extended along the entire line. It was a severe struggle. The 5th Prussians fought at Woerth, the 11th Prussians near Elsasshausen. In his strong position on and near the heights of Froschwiller, the enemy offered us a most intense resistance. The 1st Bavarian Corps reached Gorsdorff, but could not lay hold of the enemy fast enough; the 2d Bavarian had to exchange the exhausted troops of the Division Bothmer, who had spent their ammunition in the fierce fights of the morning, for the Division Walther. While the Division Bothmer fell back, the Brigade Scleich of the Division Walther marched upon Langen-Salzbach. The Wurtemburg Division approached Gunstett.

"At 2 o'clock fresh orders were given.

The Wurtemburg Division was to turn towards Reichshofen by way of Ebersbach, to threaten the enemy's line of retreat. The 1st Bavarian was to attack at once and dislodge the enemy from his position at Froschwiller and in the neighboring vineyards. Between 2 and 3 o'clock the enemy, bringing fresh troops into the field, and advancing with consummate bravery, assumed the offensive against the 5th and 11th Prussian Corps. But all his assaults were beaten off. Thus the fight was briskly going on at Woerth, neither party making much progress, till at length the brilliant attack of the 1st Bavarian Corps at Gorsdorff, and of the 1st Wurtemburg Brigade on the extreme left at Ebersbach, decided the fate of the day.

"Towards the close of the battle the French attempted a grand cavalry charge against the 5th and 11th Corps, especially against the artillery of these troops. Our artillery awaited them in a stationery position, and repulsed them with severe loss. The infantry did so likewise. This last experiment having failed, the enemy, at 4 o'clock, evacuated Froschwiller, and retreated through the mountain passes in the direction of Bitche. The cavalry of all our divisions were despatched in pursuit.

"The cavalry division which, on account of the difficult ground, which allowed little scope for its manœuvres, had been left at Schonberg, was ordered, at 3½ o'clock to advance to Gunstett. On the morning of the 7th this cavalry corps began the pursuit in the direction of Ingweiler and Bronstweiler. All the troops who had taken part in the engagement bivouacked on the battle-field, the cavalry at Gunstett, the Baden Division at Sauerburg.

"Our losses are great. The enemy lost 5,000 unwounded prisoners, thirty guns, six mitrailleuses, and two eagles. The enemy's troops arrayed against us were General MacMahon's army, and the 2d and 3d Divisions of the 6th Corps."

SAARBRUCK RETAKEN.

The town of Saarbruck was retaken by the First Prussian Army Corps, under command of General Steinmetz, on the afternoon of August 6th, 1870.

THE PRUSSIAN PIONEERS.

HOW THEIR RECONNOITRING PARTIES ARE COMPOSED.

The French attribute their want of success to the splendid manner in which the Prussians reconnoitre with the uhlans, and the completeness of their spy system, which keeps them perfectly acquainted with every stir made by their antagonists.

On the subject of the Prussian *eclaireurs*, I append the following well-written account of the manner in which they go to work. The writer begins by saying:

The qualities inherent in French nature are impetuosity, dash, and courage, but these characteristics, which Europe does not hesitate to proclaim, often carry in their wake a certain inattention. The qualities, on the other hand, peculiar to the German character, are reflection, prudence, and method. These sometimes produce slowness of attack, but they leave nothing to chance. From this aggregate of qualities and defects it results that the Prussian army is admirably well informed, and the French are scarcely so at all. Was anything known of the enormous forces which Prince Frederick Charles and the Crown Prince had accumulated on the Saar, and who bore down the two corps of General Frossard and Marshal MacMahon? The Prussians understand and practice using scouts in a campaign. The general who is confronted by a corps which he is to watch and fight chooses a clever and determined officer. A small troop is confided to him of from fifteen to twenty select horsemen, uhlans, or hussars. The officer, in his turn, takes into the band some soldiers of the landwehr, both upon the very frontier of the country which he is to reconnoitre, and which his business, his relations, and his habits allured him to visit in every sense. This man, who has a mission of confidence and honor, advances to the front, musket in hand, eye watchful, and ear attentive. He has been told what point is to be reached, which spot is marked in pencil on an excellent map, which the officer carries about him. The place which is to be reconnoitred is often twenty to thirty kilometres distant from the Prussian lines, in the very centre of the enemy's territory. Behind the first horseman, who has orders to advance very slowly, following hollows, dells, and sometimes the highway, sometimes also pushing forward across the fields, two other riders come at two hundred paces off. Further away, at the same distance from them, comes the officer, followed by eight or ten horsemen, charged to protect him, if necessary. Two other riders are further away, whom a last soldier is following at two hundred paces. This column, moving on silently, occupies the space of a kilometre. If the horseman who leads is surprised, a shot gives alarm to the rest of the band, and the riders ahead and behind have orders to depart at full gallop, and to follow any direction that is safest. The officer alone and his escort go on ahead to reconnoitre with whom they have to do, and to see what is passing, after which they all leave at full speed. Even in case of ambush, it is almost impossible that two or three riders should not be able to return safely to headquarters, and the Prussians then know at once what force they have before them, and on what point it is posted.

King William sent the following dispatch to the Queen:

"Good news. A great victory has been won by our Fritz. God be praised for his mercy. We captured 4,000 prisoners, thirty guns, two standards, and six mitrailleuses. MacMahon, during the fight, was heavily reenforced from the main army. The contest was very severe, and lasted from eleven in the morning until nine at night, when the French retreated, leaving the field to us. Our losses were heavy."

On Saturday, August 6, the French were turned back on their entire line, and commenced to retreat toward the interior of France. The French had commenced an advance from Saarbruck, which they had held since the famous battle of three divisions against three companies of Prussians, but having to fall back they burned that rich and unprotected town, and in withdrawing spread conflagration by throwing hot shot into it.

The heads of the Prussian columns approached the Saar on the 5th. Gen. Kamers found the enemy to the west of Saarbruck in strong position in the mountains near Spiehren, and immediately attacked him. Following the sound of the cannon portions of the divisions of Barnakow and Stupnagel came up. Gen. Goeben took command, and after a very severe fight, the position occupied by Gen. Frossard was taken by assault. Gen. Francois and Col. Reuter are among the wounded. Gen. Francois died the next day.

After the battle of Saarbruck, a Westphalian, going about to help the wounded, came upon a soldier of the Prussian infantry, who had been shot through the body, and was leaning heavily against a wall. "Will you drink, comrade?" asked the Westphalian. Pale and faint, the poor fellow shook his head, and feebly indicated that he would like his lips to be moistened. When this had been done, he asked in a whisper whether the Westphalian could write. The latter at once took out his pocket-book, when the dying man, "with brightening eye," dictated the words, "Dear mother, farewell," adding the address. At this moment the Westphalian was called by a second wounded man. When he returned he found that his first friend had fallen back and died.

An extract from another letter, which I received lately:—(ED.)

"The glory of war has a different aspect when we view it in the dim light of a hospital ward, with hundreds of our fellow-creatures with bleeding and shattered limbs about us, and the winged Victory should be painted with crimson wings—wings dyed red with human gore. The loss of blood from some of the patients was simply enormous, and the six miles' journey from the field of battle must have been very trying to the poor fellows, who bore their pain with wonderful fortitude and patience, the less seriously wounded assisting in undressing, and in otherwise helping their more unfortunate brethren. Occasionally you hear a cry of 'Mon Dieu! Mon Dieu!' and one poor fellow, with a ball right through his lungs, is gurgling out an anguished gasp for the absent doctor. Poor fellow! I fear the only doctor who can do him any good is that grand curer of all evils, Dr. Death.

"We turn to the right and are soon on the crown of the hill, and here, O God! what

MARSHAL CANROBERT.
Marſchall Canrobert.

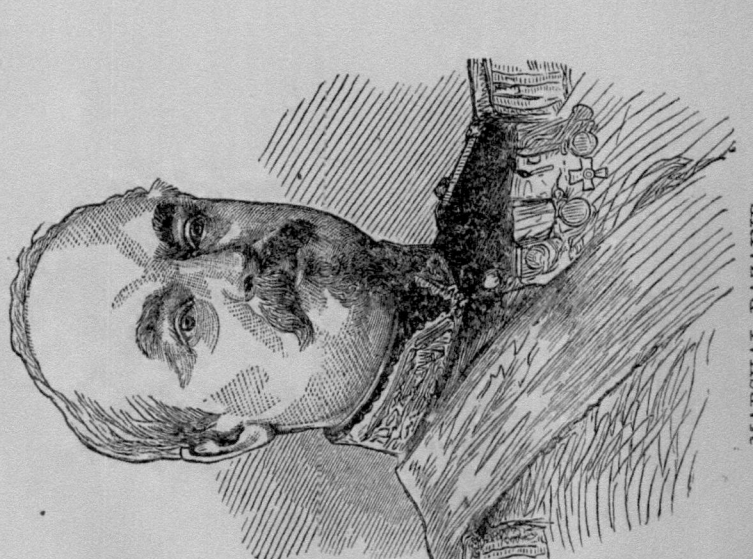

MARSHAL BAZAINE.
Marſchall Bazaine.

a sickening sight awaits us. There, in front, is a clean even line of dead Frenchmen, three deep, laid out with military regularity. As they stood in line so they fell, almost all shot through the head. Most of them have fallen forward on their faces, their arms extended, some with their fingers on the trigger they never had time to pull. Some few have reeled backwards, and there is a smashed and battered face turned towards heaven.

"There is another there whose face is half shot away. Surely it must be fancy—but no, it moves, and then it flashes to our mind that there may still be some living here, and we have a duty to do in which a neutral may engage, and we go up to him. Yes, poor fellow, he still lives, though it would almost, it seems, be the greater mercy to end that life of pain at once than attempt to save the battered remains of life he, should he live, will have to carry about with him. But as he lives something must be done. The question is, what ? Not a French soldier is near, not a French doctor, not one of that multitudinous and polyglot assemblage who sport their white 'Drassards' with so much complacency in Metz. There is no help for it but to go right up to the Prussians there, and ask in God's name for their help for a wounded enemy. This is done, and with truest noble-heartedness a party of their own men and a cart are sent off with us for any wounded men we may find. Here and there we pick up another still breathing soldier, and consign him to the kindly hands of those who a few hours ago were just as anxious to kill him as they are willing now to save. This is the scene of the hottest part of the fight, and the dead lie thickly around. Scarcely, however, do we see a Prussian. They have already removed them, and their wounded have been cared for some hours ago.

"There lies a Chasseur de Vincennes. Surely he must be living, his color is so good; nor can he be deeply wounded. Why, then, is he so still ? Hearing French voices near him he looks up, pretending to awake out of sleep. For about sixteen hours he has lain there in mortal funk—no other word will do—and the wretched coward appeals to us to deliver him from the hands of the Prussians. I am sorely tempted to call them up and give the wretched animal into their custody; but then they would have to keep him, and he certainly is not worth his keep, so the counsels of my French friend prevail, and we pick the creature up. He is so stiff from his seeming death that he can scarcely stand. We call a couple of peasants, and he leans on them as though seriously wounded; and thus we lead him away.

"A well-to-do-looking farmer stops us and tells us there are some wounded up by the wood yonder; so across the fields we go, and here we find a heap of dead, and amongst them three poor soldiers, who have lain there since about 3 o'clock yesterday, unable to move, without a particle of food, or, above

all, without a drop of water. One of us goes back to Borny to seek some help, whilst the other stays and tries to give some relief to the cramped and stiffened limbs, or at any rate a few kindly words of hope and encouragement. An hour's waiting brings a long country cart, with plenty of straw in it, and we lifted the poor fellows into the shaky vehicle, and jolt them over the fields as gently as possible, yet still with horrible agony to their crushed and bleeding limbs. At last we reach, the road, and progress is somewhat easier, passing on our way we see another poor fellow whom it would be dangerous to lift into such a cart as ours. He needs those beautiful stretchers which are so scientifically constructed, but which are all where the doctors are, in Metz, doing nothing. Nor can we do anything for him now, poor fellow. He would probably die on the road, and meanwhile would cause an increased agony to those we are already transporting. All we can do is to build a bower of branches to keep off the blazing sun, and send word when we get to Metz to have him brought in if he should live that long."

THE BATTLE OF FORBACH.

The official account of the action at Forbach is as follows :

"On the forenoon of August 6, the 7th Corps d'Armee pushed its vanguard to Herchenbach, 1¼ German miles northwest of Saarbruck, with outposts stretching as far as the river Saar. The preceding night the enemy had evacuated its position on the drilling-ground of Saarbruck.

"Toward noon the Cavalry Division under General Rheinhaben passed through the town. Two squadrons formed the van. The moment they reached the highest point of the drilling-ground, and became visible to spectators on the south, they were fired at from the hills near Spicheren.

"The drilling-ground ridge overhangs a deep valley stretching towards Forbach and Spicheren, and bordered on the other side by the steep and partly wooded height named after the latter village. These hills, rising in almost perpendicular ascent several hundred feet above the valley, form a natural fortress, which needed no addition from art to be all but impregnable. Like so many bastions, the mountains project into the valley, facing it on all sides, and affording the strongest imaginable position for defence. French officers who were taken prisoners on this spot confess to having smiled at the idea of the Prussians attacking them in this stronghold. There was not a man in the 2d French Corps who was not persuaded in his own mind that to attempt the Spicheren hills must lead to the utter annihilation of the besiegers.

"Between 12 and 1 the 14th Division arrived at Saarbruck. Immediately proceeding south, it encountered a strong force of the enemy in the valley between Saarbruck and Spicheren, and opened fire forthwith. Upon this General Frossard, who was in the act of withdrawing a portion of his troops when the Prussians arrived, turned round and reoccupied the Spicheren hills with his entire force. A division of the 3d Corps, under General Bazaine, came up in time to support him.

"The 14th Division at first had to deal with far superior numbers. To limit the attack to the enemy's front would have been useless. General von Kamecke, therefore, while engaging the front, also attempted to turn the left flank of the enemy by Stiring; but the five battalions he could spare for this operation were too weak to make an impression upon the much stronger numbers of the French. Two successive attacks on his left were repulsed by General Frossard. Toward 3 o'clock, when all the troops of the division were under fire, the engagement assumed a very sharp and serious aspect.

"Eventually, however, the roar of the cannon attracted several other Prussian detachments. The division under General von Barkenow was the first to be drawn to the spot. Two of its batteries came dashing up at full speed to relieve their struggling comrades. They were promptly followed by the 40th Infantry, under Colonel Rex, and three squadrons of the 9th Hussars. At this moment the vanguard of the 5th Division was espied on the Winterberg Hill. General Stulpnagel, whose van had been stationed at Sultzbach the same morning, had been ordered by General von Alvensleben to march his entire division in the direction from which the sound of cannon proceeded. Two batteries advanced in a forced march on the high road. The infantry were partly sent by rail from Nuenkirchen to Saarbruck.

"At about 3.30 o'clock the Division Kamecke had been sufficiently reinforced to enable General von Goeben, who had arrived in the meantime and assumed the command, to make a vigorous onslaught on the enemy's front. The chief aim of the attack was the wooded portion of the declivity. The 40th Infantry, supported on its right by troops of the 14th Division, and on its left by four battalions of the 5th Division, made the assault. A reserve was formed of some battalions of the 5th and 16th Divisions, as they came up.

"The charge was a success. The wood was occupied, the enemy expelled. Penetrating further, always on the ascent, the troops pushed the French before them as far as the southern outskirts of the wood. Here the French made a stand, and, combining the three arms of the service for a united attack, endeavored to retrieve the day. But our infantry were not to be shaken. At this juncture the artillery of the 5th Division accomplished a rare and most daring feat. Two batteries literally clambered up the hill of Spicheren by a narrow and precipitous mountain path. With their help a fresh attack of the enemy was repulsed. A flank attack directed against our left from Aislingen and Spicheren was warded off in time by battalions of the 5th Division stationed in reserve.

"The fighting, which for hours had been conducted with the utmost obstinacy on both sides, now reached its climax. Once more the enemy, superior still in numbers, rallied his entire forces for a grand and impetuous charge. It was his third attack after we had occupied the wood. But, like the preceding ones, this last effort was shortened by the imperturbable calmness of our infantry and artillery. Like waves dashing and breaking against a rock, the enemy's battalions were scattered by our gallant troops. After this last failure the enemy beat a rapid retreat; fifty-two French battalions, with the artillery of an entire corps, stationed in an almost unassailable position, had thus been defeated by twenty-seven Prussian battalions, supported by but the artillery of one division. It was a brilliant victory, indeed. We had everything against us—numbers, guns, and the nature of the locality; yet we prevailed.

"Darkness fast setting in afforded its valuable aid to the enemy in effecting his retreat. To cover this backward movement, the French artillery were stationed on the hills skirting the battle-field on the south, where they kept up a continuous but harmless fire for a considerable time.

"The ground was too difficult for the cavalry to take any part in the action. Nevertheless, the fruits of the victory were very remarkable. The corps under General Frossard, being entirely demoralized, dispersed. The road it took in its hasty flight was marked by numerous wagons with provisions and clothing; the woods were filled with hosts of stragglers, wandering about in a purposeless way, and large stores and quantities of goods of every description fell into our hands.

"While the battle was raging at Spicheren Hill, the 13th Division crossed the Saar at Werden, occupied Forbach, seized vast magazines of food and clothing, and thus forced General Frossard, whose retreat was covered by two divisions of General Bazaine, which had come up for the purpose, to withdraw to the southwest and leave free the road to St. Avold.

"The losses were very serious on both sides. The 5th Division alone has 230 dead, and about 1,800 wounded. The 12th Infantry has 32 officers and 800 men dead or wounded; next to this the 40th, 8th, 48th, 39th, and 74th have suffered most. The batteries, too, have encountered terrible loss. The number of killed and wounded on the enemy's side was at least equal to our own. The unwounded prisoners in our hands already exceed 2,000, and were increasing hourly. We have also captured forty pontoons, and the tents of the camp."

THE BATTLES AROUND METZ.

Meanwhile the valley of the Moselle had become the scene of stirring events. The

Prussian right, as already stated, had followed the retreating French under Frossard after the battle of Forbach until they were close upon the Moselle, in which threatening position they awaited the arrival of the Prussian centre, under Prince Frederick Charles. The latter, striking the Moselle near Pont-a-Mousson, crossed that stream on Sunday, August 14, with the object of turning the French right, and cutting off communications with MacMahon, who had, as already stated, abandoned Nancy on the 13th and hastened westward towards Chalons, closely followed by the Prussian left under the Crown Prince.

The abandonment of the line of the Moselle was the first thing determined upon by Bazaine after his increased authority under the Palikao administration. On Sunday, August 14, he began the movement of his army across the Moselle, in the immediate vicinity of Metz, where he had collected it on the 12th. Before he had accomplished his purpose, however, the 1st and 7th Prussian Corps of General von Steinmetz's command fell upon his rear, and a serious engagement ensued, at the end of which the entire French army had succeeded in effecting the passage of the stream. But, while the Prussians suffered a loss quite out of proportion to that inflicted on the French, the westward movement of the latter was materially delayed, and the first object of the Prussians practically accomplished.

On Monday, the 15th, the army of General von Steinmetz having crossed the Moselle, the hostile forces were engaged principally in manœuvring for position; but there appears to have been two distinct and determined engagements, and on the following day, the 16th, there was a protracted and bloody contest. The fighting was continued on the 17th, and the struggle for the possession of the roads from Metz to Verdun culminated on the 18th, in the great battle of Gravelotte. By this time the original positions of the hostile armies were reversed, the Prussians facing east and the French west. The final struggle lasted from 10 o'clock in the morning until 9 in the evening. It was the battle of Sadowa, fought over again. At the opening, the junction between Prince Frederick Charles and General von Steinmetz had not been effected. The French were between two fires, but that of Von Steinmetz did not become effective until evening, when he swept down from the northeast, and, turning the right flank of the enemy, decided the fortunes of the field. Bazaine was thrown back on Metz, his communications with Paris were cut off, and the Crown Prince was left at liberty to pursue his advance towards the capital, without the danger of encountering any opposition other than could be presented by MacMahon's demoralized force and the new levies that were being gathered at Chalons.

THE BATTLE OF GRAVELOTTE.

One of the most important battles of the war in France was that which took place near Metz, on Thursday, the 18th of August, between the forces under command of Marshal Bazaine and the armies of the Prince Royal of Prussia and General Steinmetz, the result of which was the penning up of the French within the fortifications of that stronghold. From the hill the entire sweep of the Prussian and French centre could be seen, and a considerable part of their wings, and where, at the time, were the headquarters of the King. The great representative men of Prussia, soldiers and statesmen, were standing on the ground watching the conflict just begun. Among them were the King, Bismarck, General von Moltke, Prince Frederick Charles, Prince Carl, Prince Adalbert, and Adjutant Kranski. Lieutenant-General Sheridan, of the United States army, was also present. At the moment the French were making a most desperate effort to hold on to the last bit of the Verdun road—that between Rezonville and Gravelotte, or that part of Gravelotte which in some maps is called St. Marcel. The struggle was desperate but unavailing, for every one man in the French army had two to cope with, and their line was already beginning to waver. Soon it was plain that this wing, the French right, was withdrawing to a new position. This was swiftly taken up under cover of a continuous fire of their artillery from the heights beyond the village. The movement was made in good order, and the position, which was reached at one o'clock and thirty minutes, would have been pronounced impregnable by nine out of ten military men. When once this movement had been effected, the French retreating from the pressure of the Prussian artillery fire, and the Prussians as rapidly advancing, the battle-field was no longer about Rezonville, but had been transferred and pushed forward to Gravelotte, the junction of the two branching roads to Verdun. The fields in front of that village were completely covered by the Prussian reserves, and interminable lines of soldiers were steadily marching onward, disappearing into the village, and emerging on the other side of it with flaming volleys.

This second battle-field was less extensive than the first, and brought the opposing forces into fearfully close quarters. The peculiarity of it is that it consists of two heights intersected by a deep ravine. This woody ravine is over 100 feet deep, and at the top some 300 yards wide. The side of the chasm next to Gravelotte, where the Prussians stood, is much lower than the other side, which gradually ascends to a great height. From their commanding eminence the French held their enemies fairly beneath them, and poured upon them scorching fire. The French stood their ground and died—the Prussians stood their ground and died—both by hundreds, I had almost said thousands.

This, for an hour or two that seemed ages, so constant was the slaughter. The hill where I stood commanded chiefly the conflict behind the village and to the south of it. The Prussian reinforcements, coming up on their right, filed out of the Bois des Ognons; and it was at that point, as they marched on to the field, that one could perhaps get the best idea of the magnitude of this invading army now in the heart of France. There was no break whatever for four hours in the march of men out of that wood. Birnam Wood advancing to Dunsinane Hill was not a more ominous sight to Macbeth than these men of General Goeben's army to Bazaine, shielded as they were by the woods till they were fairly within range and reach of their enemy's guns. So the French must have felt; for between 4 and 5 o'clock they concentrated upon that spot their heaviest fire, massing all available guns, and shelling the woods unremittingly. Their fire reached the Prussian lines and tore through them; and, though the men were steady, it was a test to which no General cares to subject his troops long. Once out from under the trees the Prussians advanced at double-quick. The French guns had not lost the range of the wood, nor of the ground in front. Seen at a distance, through a powerful glass, the brigade was a huge serpent bending with the undulation of the field. But it left a dark track behind it, and the glass resolved the dark track into falling and dying and dead men. Many of those who had fallen leaped up again and ran forward a little way, striving still to go on with their comrades. Of those who went backward instead of forward there were few, though many fell as they painfully endeavored to follow the advance.

Now and then the thick cloud which hung over the battle-field would open a little and drift away on the wind, and then the French could be seen, sorely tried. To get a better view of this part of the field, the correspondent went forward about half a mile, and from this new stand-point found himself not far from Malmaison. The French line on the hills was still unbroken, and, to all appearances, they were having the best of the battle. But this appearance was due, perhaps, to the fact that the French were more clearly visible on their broad height, and fighting with such singular obstinacy. They plainly silenced a Prussian battery now and then. But the Prussian line also was strengthened by degrees on this northern point. Infantry and artillery were brought up; and from far in the rear—away, seemingly, in the direction of Verneville—shot and shell began reaching the French ranks. These were the men and these were the guns of Steinmetz, who there and then effected his junction with the army of Prince Frederick Charles, and completed the investment of Metz to the northwest.

Steinmetz was able to extend his line gradually further and further, until the French were outflanked and began to be threatened, as it appeared, with an attack on the rear of their extreme right wing. So long as the smoke from the Prussian guns hovered only over their front, the French clung to their position. The distance from headquarters to where the Prussian flank attack stretched forward was great; and, to add to the difficulty of clearly seeing the battle, the darkness was coming on. The puffs of smoke from the French guns mingled with the flashes, brightening as the darkness increased, receded gradually. The pillars of cloud and flame from the north as gradually and steadily approached. With that advance the French fire every moment grew more slack. It was not far from nine o'clock when the ground was yielded finally on the north, and the last shots fired on that terrible evening were heard in that direction.

So the battle raged with fluctuating success, until about half-past eight or nine in the evening, when the decisive blow was struck. When the battle of Gravelotte had actually ended, it was known that the Prussians held the strong heights beyond the Bois de Vaux, which command the surrounding country to the limits of artillery range from Metz; that two great Prussian armies lay across the only road by which Bazaine could march to Paris for its relief, or for his own escape; that a victory greater than that of Sunday, and more decisive than the triumph of Tuesday, had been won; and that, in all probability, the French army, which had fought as valiantly and as vainly as before, was now hopelessly shut up in the fortress.

PARIS IN PERIL.

From first to last the engagements around Metz were claimed by the French as victories, but the only foundation for this claim consisted in the alleged fact that the Prussians lost the greater number of men in killed and wounded, the truth of which it is impossible, even at this late day, to ascertain. The attempt of Bazaine to transfer his army from the neighborhood of Metz, however, was certainly foiled; and while a portion of the united armies of Prince Frederick Charles and General von Steinmetz was detached to watch the French, the remainder were pushed forward towards the still advancing army of the Crown Prince.

By the time that General Trochu assumed command of Paris, the capital was fairly persuaded that a siege was inevitable, and every nerve was strained to prepare a determined and desperate reception for the enemy, in case they should advance to the gates of the capital. As already stated, this contingency appeared imminent, for parties of Prussian cavalry approached to within forty or fifty miles of Paris, and at one time the eastern terminus of the railroad to Chalons and Rheims was fixed at Chateau-Thierry, but 45 miles from the capital and only half the distance to Chalons. General Trochu assumed the command of Paris in a proclamation issued on August 18th, and the preparations for defence were steadily pressed forward. Laborers by the thousands swarmed upon the fortifications; 3000 cannon, according to the French reports, were mounted upon the walls and exterior forts, manned by 15,000 well-trained cannoniers, taken for the most part from the navy; a motley army of 200,000 men, in which the regular element numbered scarcely 20,000, was assembled in and around the city; portions of the Bois de Boulogne and Bois de Vincennes were destroyed, to give the artillery an unimpeded command of the approaches, a large number of houses in proximity to the fortifications being demolished for the same purpose; immense quantities of provisions were stored in the city, and hordes of beeves, sheep and swine collected; the country in front of the advancing Prussians was ordered to be laid waste, and the bridges over the streams to be destroyed on their approach.

The general management of these preparations was entrusted to a Committee of Defence, on which were General Trochu, Marshal Vaillana, Admiral Rigault de Genouilly, Minister Jerome David. On the 23d of August, the members of the party of the Left demanded that nine deputies be added to this committee. The Ministry at first resisted this demand, but on the 26th Count Napoleon Daru, who had preceded the Duke de Gramont as Minister of Foreign Affairs under M. Ollivier, and two Senators were added, and on the 27th it was still further strengthened by the name of the veteran Orleanist M. Thiers, to the general satisfaction of people of all parties.

MacMAHON'S EFFORT TO RESCUE BAZAINE.

Paris being thus occupied in preparations to take care of herself, MacMahon halted in his retreat at Chalons, and made a venture from that point towards Mézières, with the intention of effecting a junction with Bazaine. The camp at Chalons was broken up on the 22d of August, and burned on the 25th, a portion of the new levies departing for the front with MacMahon, while the Garde Mobile of Paris, in which signs of insubordination were manifest, were marched back to the capital immediately after the departure of Trochu. The army of MacMahon had been spread out in front of Chalons and Rheims for some days, but was finally concentrated in a general movement towards the northeast, the headquarters reaching Rethel, midway between Rheims and Mézières, on August 25. While these movements were under way to the west of the Meuse, Bazaine himself was repeatedly reported as having broken through the Prussian lines around Metz, and succeeded in reopening his communications with MacMahon and Paris. A small portion of his army, which had been cut off from the main body during the prolonged series of engagements around Metz, apparently succeeded in accomplishing this object, but the

escaping force was an inconsiderable one, if it had any existence at all, and Bazaine remained shut up under the guns of Metz until the final blow fell upon MacMahon at Sedan. From the morning of August 31st until noon on the following day, Bazaine appears to have made a last desperate attempt at piercing the Prussian lines, but a portion of Prince Frederick Charles' army, under Gen. Von Mantenffel, successfully resisted the attempt, and he was again hurled back upon the fortress of Metz, the engagement, which was severe as well as protracted, being styled the battle of Noiseville.

The French army has been out-generalled and out-fought. At the beginning of the campaign all the conditions were in the Emperor's favor; but Von Moltke beat him in manœuvring as Von Steinmetz beat Frossard, and the Crown Prince decidedly beat MacMahon. The strategy of the Prussian left was indeed in beautiful contrast with all the French movements up to this time. In actual conflict the superiority of the Prussians seems to have been equally marked. There have been fair standup fights and headlong charges, and the Germans have shown, in addition to their characteristic steadiness and obstinacy, all that *élan* which is supposed to be the distinguishing merit of the French.

I shall not wonder if European armies learn the same truth which was so clearly shown in our war of the Rebellion, that young men are the best generals. The Crown Prince of Prussia, who has the chief glory of the defeat of the French army, is not yet thirty-nine years old, and before he was thirty-five he had made himself a great name at Sadowa. Prince Frederick Charles, the King's nephew, who commands the Prussian right, and is esteemed the ablest of all King William's generals, is forty-two years old. Most of the fighting at Sadowa was done by his army. Nearly all the French leaders are old men.

THE DOWNFALL OF OLLIVIER.

All Germany was thrown into a blaze of enthusiasm by these startling victories, and all France was overwhelmed with dismay. The news of the disasters reached Paris on the 7th, and that turbulent city was seized with a paroxysm of rage and defiance. The first and foremost object of condemnation was the Ministry, through whose incompetency the people believed disaster had fallen upon the army. The Corps Législatif was called together on the 9th, and a terrible scene was enacted on the opening of the session. Vast multitudes of people surrounded the hall wherein the Deputies assembled, which was protected by a large force of regular troops under Marshal Baraguay d'Hilliers, the commander of Paris. These troops were greeted with derisive shouts of "To the frontier!" and a serious encounter between them and the people was barely averted.

But the passions of the populace were soon gratified by the result of the proceedings within the hall. When M. Ollivier ascended the tribune and announced that the deputies had been called together before the situation of the country was compromised, M. Jules Favre cried out, "Descend from the tribune; this is shameful!" Protestations of ability on the part of the Ministry to save the country were unavailing. M. Favre demanded that the Chamber should at once assume the management of affairs through an executive committee of fifteen members, a proposition which the president, M. Schneider, refused to entertain, because of its revolutionary and unconstitutional character. A terrible scene of disorder ensued in which there were several personal conflicts. Finally M. Ollivier made a stand by resisting the demand for the order of the day, but it was carried in his face, and after a short recess he announced the resignation of the Ministry, and the selection by the Empress Regent of the Count de Palikao as the head of the new Cabinet.

The new Premier selected for himself the portfolio of War, and on the following day announced as the names of his colleagues the Prince de la Tour d'Auvergne, Foreign Affairs; Henri Chevreau, Interior; Admiral Regault de Genouilly, (the old incumbent, and the only member of the Ollivier Ministry retained,) Marine; Pierre Magne, Finance; Jerome David, Public Works; Jules Brame, Public Instruction; M. Grand-Perret, Justice; Clement Duvernois, Agriculture and Commerce; and M. Busson-Billault, President of the Council of State. The new Ministry, without exception, belonged to the extreme Bonapartist party, the party which had been overthrown to make way for the so-called "responsible" Ministry, at the head of which Ollivier had been placed. But from the outset they seemed to possess the confidence of the people, and they went to work with a will to repair the shattered fortunes of France. M. Magne, who had frequently been at the head of the Department of Finance before, and had been the instrument through which Napoleon had negotiated nearly all the loans of his reign, introduced and carried a measure for a new war loan of 2,500,000,000 francs, and Imperialists and Republicans vied with each other in advocating measures for the placing of every able-bodied Frenchman under arms. The Republicans, lead by Favre, Gambetta, and Keratry, however, indulged in daily assaults upon the head of the Government, denouncing the Emperor for meddling with the management of the army, and charging the majority with the responsibility of having entered upon a war for which the country was not prepared.

Marshal Bazaine was placed in chief command of the army; Le Bœuf, who, as previous Minister of War and subsequently Major-General or Chief-of-Staff of the army, was justly held accountable in great part for the Prussian victories, was deposed; General Trochu, who had enjoyed a high reputation as a soldier, without having an opportunity to display his ability, was named as Le Bœuf's successor, but sent at first to the camp at Chalons to organize the new levies, and from that position called back to Paris, on August 17, as Military Governor of the capital, in place of Marshal Baraguay d'Hilliers; and throughout France, as well as in Paris, there was such an expression of determination to repel the invader, that the entire nation appeared at last to have realized the magnitude of its peril and risen to an equality with the situation.

THE PERIL OF PARIS.

THE POSITION OF THE CAPITAL FROM A FRENCH STANDPOINT—ITS DEFENSES—THE VULNERABLE POINT—HOW THE SIEGE MUST BE CONDUCTED.

Paris is not an ordinary fortress, it is a vast intrenched camp, defended by more than half a million of men, and protected by a wall of circumvallation eighteen miles in circumference, defended by ninety-three bastions, and fortified in accordance with the most perfect rules of the art. Nor is this all. These strong defenses are themselves defended, at distances varying from one and a quarter miles to four and a half miles, by a girdle of fifteen detached forts, provided with seven great outworks, flanking each other, and forming a second inclosure of thirty miles in circumference, whose powerful artillery can sweep everything before it at a distance of six miles. Paris, finally, is defended by the Seine, by the Marne, and by a circular railroad with which all the lines in France are connected, and which renders it possible to convey troops with great rapidity to the points menaced in the outer or inner line of fortifications. A place of this extent can be subjected neither to a proper siege nor to an investment complete enough to shut out reinforcements and supplies. It can, then, only be attacked at a given point, and the question remains what is the most vulnerable point of this immense circuit.

The forts of the east—Romainville, Noesy, Rosny, Nogent, and Vincennes—are very advantageously situated on the summit of a plateau, partly covered by the Marne. They form a formidable line of defence, and it would be imprudent—so the Prussian officer formally declares—to attempt an attack at this point. Nor must an attack be thought of on the Fort Charenton, situated to the south of the preceding, because, after its capture, it would be necessary to cross the Marne, under the triple fire of the forts of Vincennes, Ivry, and inner works of Paris. To the south of Paris and to the west of Charenton are situated the forts of Ivry and Bicetre, but the siege works could only be executed under the fire of the adjoining forts. The other forts on the south—Montrouge, Vannes, and Issy—rising on the steep heights which extend from Sceaux to Versailles, are difficult of attack, and the same may be said of the citadel of Mont Valerien, the only fort which

GEN. FROSSARD.
General Frossard.

PRINCE IMPERIAL.
Kronprinz von Frankreich.

defends Paris on the west. Mont Valerien is situated at a distance of five miles from the fort of Issy, but counting from the latter, Paris is doubly covered by the Seine, which first flows to the northeast, forms a bend, joins the forts of St. Denis, and then directs its course to the southwest, parallel to and slightly distant from the first curve. Exactly in the middle of these bendings of the river is situated Mont Valerien. The French could launch vessels upon the Seine, armed with guns of heavy calibre, which would inflict cruel havoc on the besiegers. The river Seine, from Issy to St. Cloud, and beyond Mont Valerien, is besides protected by obstacles in the shape of wooded heights and country villas, which could easily be adapted for purposes of defense.

The efforts of the besiegers must therefore be directed upon St. Denis, and here we borrow the exact words of the Prussian Lieutenant-Colonel:—"For a German besieging army, the points of attack of the fortifications of Paris are naturally the north and northeast. In the first place they are the weakest, for the east front is partly covered by the Marne, and those of the south and west are the strongest, and their attack might compromise the line of retreat of the besiegers, upon which the French army of reserve would not fail to operate. So as not to expose themselves to have this cut, the besiegers must choose the north as the point of attack, for their army of observation ought to cover the lines of retreat which will follow the course of the Meuse and the Seine, as they could also be able to restore the railroads from Strasburg and Muhlhouse which run along these valleys. These roads would also serve for the transport of siege material from the Rhine fortresses, if the French positions captured had not already furnished it. In any case the material must be of the very heaviest calibre. Admitting that the German army of observation should be stronger than the French army of reserve, and that the latter, held at a distance from Paris, was unable to interrupt the siege, St. Denis should be the first point of attack. Its capture would, in fact, permit of an advance towards Montmartre on the wall of circumvallation, without being exposed to the flank and rear fire of the outer forts. Only those who start from the Seine need be regarded with any apprehension.

The three forts of St. Denis and that of Aubervilliers will be simultaneously besieged, and a less serious attack will be made on the other forts facing west. The siege will then assume the same character as that of Sebastopol, and the siege works will have to be undertaken at the same time against a line of fortifications extending over several leagues. St. Denis is situated on the right bank of the Seine, which, at this point, doubles back on its course, and forms a tongue of land whence the siege works might be taken in flank and rear. Its occupation by the besiegers becomes thus a necessity. It is difficult, but not impossible, if the Seine is crossed in the neighborhood of Argenteuil. The besiegers will then be able to command the citadel of Mont Valerien, situated upon the second tongue of land, to destroy the railroad communication of the left bank of the Seine with Paris, and to cover the attack upon St. Denis. A bridge thrown over the Seine would place them in communication with the troops operating on the right bank.

In order to execute this daring plan, the Prussian strategist assigns to each corps of the invading army the place it ought to occupy, and the part it will be called upon to play in the general plan of operations. He places 50,000 men before the three forts of St. Denis, and on the tongue of land formed by the Seine between St. Denis and Mount Valerien. He masses 20,000 men on the north at St. Denis in order to cover the siege of this point, and to reinforce the corps isolated on both banks of the Seine. These 70,000 men are to find their material of preparation to the north of St. Denis, or in the forest of Bondy. We might concentrate, he adds, 30,000 men in this forest, 20,000 at Bourget, behind La Molette, and 30,000 at Neuilly-sur-Marne, in order to occupy the routes from Metz and from Coulommiers, and sustain the besieging corps at St. Denis. The 20,000 men at Bourget would menace the fort of Aubervilliers, and might be able to besiege it. They would be scarcely two and a half miles distant from St. Denis, and would form, along with the troops posted at this point, a mass of 90,000 men. These, united with the 30,000 established in the forest of Bondy, at two and a half miles from Bourget, would be able to offer in this forest a very energetic resistance in the event of being compelled to retreat, or if they wished to act against the sallies in force of the besieged, to which they would necessarily be exposed. On the other hand, the 30,000 men posted at Neuilly, on the right bank of the Marne, will be able to occupy the hill to the east of the fort of Rosny, and to undertake a series of attacks, not very formidable, it is true, against the forts facing east, as well as to form, with the 30,000 men, in the forest of Bondy, an army of 60,000, which could secure the path of retreat. Other 30,000 men should be placed between Neuilly-sur-Marne and Villeneuve-sur-Seine, in order to observe the roads which start from the confluence of the Seine and the Marne towards the east. Bridges established on the Marne would place these 30,000 men in communication with the troops established on the right bank at Neuilly. The besieging army would then number 180,000 men, but to besiege Paris this is not sufficient. To protect adequately the besiegers, a great army of observation is required. This *role* is assigned by the Prussian lieutenant-colonel to the 3d Army, whom he supposes to number 120,000 men, and to whom he wishes to join a 4th army, penetrating into France by way of Switzerland. On this hypothesis, the invading army would arrive before Paris with an effective strength of 400,000 men. The task of the latter divisions would be to hold the French army of relief as far from Paris as possible, to intercept supplies, and to destroy the railroads which place Paris in communication with the south and west of France.

DEPUTY JULES FAVRE.

THE MAN FOR PRESIDENT OF THE FRENCH REPUBLIC—A SKETCH OF HIS CAREER—A LIFE DEVOTED TO THE CAUSE OF LIBERTY, AND UNTAINTED WITH FANATICISM—HIS BRILLIANT POLITICAL RECORD, AND EARNEST ANTAGONISM TO BONAPARTISM IN EVERY SHAPE.

As a firm, consistent, and constant advocate for more than twenty years of Republican principles, M. Jules Favre occupies a leading position in the Corps Législatif of France. Indeed, there is but one man who has pretended to dispute with him the leadership of the true Republican party since Emile Ollivier went over to the Empire for the sake of making his futile experiment at constitutional government under a Bonaparte regime, and that man is M. Gambetta.

Gabriel Claude Jules Favre is almost twice as old as his rival, Gambetta, having been born at Lyons on March 31, 1809. In the revolution of July, 1830, which found him a student at law in Paris, he took an active part, and from that day to this, through the press, at the bar, and in the different National Assemblies, he has remained a bold, undaunted, outspoken champion of the better type of French republicanism. The independence of his character, the bitter irony of his address, and the consistent radicalism of his opinions, soon achieved for him a reputation, which has never been sullied by any compromise with Bonapartism other than the taking of the oath of allegiance to the Empire, when he finally entered the Corps Législatif. He was admitted to the bar soon after arriving at age, and during the reign of Louis Phillippe devoted himself mainly to the practice of his profession. It was not until after the Revolution of February, 1848, that he entered office for the first time. He then became Secretary-General to the Minister of the Interior, and in that capacity was called on to write the circular to the Commissioners of the Provisional Government and the famous "Bulletins" of 1848. He was soon transferred to the Under-Secretaryship for Foreign Affairs, and, being elected a member of the Assembly, voted for the prosecution of Louis Blanc and Caussidiere, for their complicity in the insurrection of June, 1848; refused to join in the vote of thanks to General Cavaignac; and resolutely opposed the expedition to Rome in December, 1848, by which Louis Napoleon incurred the hostility of the leading republicans with whom he had theretofore affiliated. He opposed the elevation of the Bonaparte adventurer to the Presidency, and after that event became his strenuous antagonist in the National Assembly. The implication of Ledru-Rollin in the plot to overthrow the Prince President rendered it necessary for the leader of the "Mountain" party to seek safety in England, after which Jules Favre succeeded to the leadership.

By the *coup d'etat* he was driven into retirement, as he refused to take the oath of allegiance to the new Constitution on being elected a member of the Counseil-General of Loire-et-Rhone. He then devoted himself for some years to his profession, and as one of the counsel of Orsini, in October, 1858, created an immense sensation by the boldness and eloquence of his defence of the reckless enthusiast who had attempted the life of the Emperor. But he entered the Corps Législatif the same year, taking the oath of allegiance to the empire which he detested; and since that time, by successive re-elections in 1863 and 1869, has signalized himself by an unswerving antagonism of the Imperial policy. He was one of the original "five" opposition members, has advocated the complete liberty of the press, opposed the "law of deportation," fought against French interference in the Italian war of independence against Austria, in 1859, and in 1864 severely assailed the ill-starred Mexican venture of the Emperor. In 1837, he published a work entitled "Contemporaneous Biography," and since that time many of his famous speeches, and several pamphlets have been given to the public in a permanent form. In August, 1860, and again in 1861, he was elected *batonnier* or president of the order of advocates at Paris, a fitting recognition of his high standing in the profession; and in May, 1867, he became a member of the French Academy.

When Napoleon showed signs of yielding something to the pressure of public opinion, after the general elections of May, 1869, M. Favre's name came to be mentioned prominently in connection with Ollivier's as the head of the responsible ministry which was about to be installed. But he soon dispelled the possibility of the scheme by declaring his dissatisfaction with the proposed "constitutional regime." "So long," he wrote in September last, "as the press is amenable to judges only, and not to a jury; so long as there is no guarantee for individual liberty; so long as elections are not free, and the mayors are not elected by the populations; so long as an enormous standing army weighs upon our budget, we should be the most contemptible people on earth if we were satisfied." So he succeeded to the position vacated by Ollivier, on the latter's accession to power.

On the 25th of June last, just before the war-cloud gathered over Europe, M. Favre delivered a famous speech in the Chamber, in which he was as unmerciful to the first empire as to the second. While supporting a proposal of the Left that the municipalities should be allowed to elect their mayors, he asserted that the inherent rights of the municipalities, recognized as early as the thirteenth century, had been stamped out by the first Napoleon. Dazzled by the glitter of his military glory, France was still under the influence of his tyrannical ideas, under the false impression that a genius had saved her from ruin, while in reality he had ruined her and annihilated her liberties. This plain speaking created a great uproar, and when Granier de Cassignac, one of the most servile tools of the third Napoleon, interrupted him with the declaration that the first Napoleon "covered France with institutions; you and your friends with ruins," M. Favre referred to the humiliation of France through foreign invasions, which would have been averted if liberty had held command of the army instead of despotism, declared that there was not a single man in the Chamber who would venture to assert that liberty existed under the first empire, and continued:—"*I am vindicating the glory of the country against the unconscious votaries of despotism, who are anxious to revive traditions which would once more bring about our degradation!*"

These stirring words, uttered scarcely three weeks before the declaration of war against Prussia, and before there was a sign of the approaching conflict, were unconsciously prophetic.

The rise of the Hohenzollern difficulty found M. Favre fully prepared to lead the assault upon the Ollivier Government. On the 8th of July, when the ministry attempted to secure a postponement of the discussion of the question, and refused to lay before the Chamber the documents relating to it, he declared that the object of delay was to afford an opportunity for stock-jobbing on the Bourse, and when the final declaration of war came, took his stand by the side of Thiers and Gambetta, and insisted upon the production of all the correspondence with Prussia, declaring that France could not make war on the authority of mere telegrams. But after the French defeat at Weissenburg, he at once urged an unflinching resistance to the invader, joining with sixteen other deputies on the 8th of August in signing a demand that all France should be armed to repel the enemy.

On the 9th the Corps Législatif was reassembled by order of the Empress, and in the exciting scene which ensued, ending in Ollivier's downfall, M. Favre played an important part. Ollivier opened the session by stating that the deputies had been called together before the situation of the country had been compromised, to which M. Favre answered that it had already been compromised by the incapacity of its chief. "Descend from the tribune," he cried out to Ollivier; "this is shameful! In spite of its government, the country is patriotic, but it is vilely ruled." He then offered resolutions for arming every able-bodied citizen of Paris on the electoral lists, and for investing in an executive committee of fifteen members the full powers of the Government for repelling foreign invasion In his speech in support of these propositions, M. Favre insisted that the Emperor should be recalled from the army, and that the only hope of saving the country was by wresting power from incapable hands that then held it. His proposition for the assumption of supreme authority by the Corps Législatif was declared by the President, the obsequious Schneider, to be revolutionary, and that functionary refused to submit it to a vote.

The Ollivier ministry were driven from power, and on the accession of the Count de Palikao, M. Favre gave the new government his cordial support in all measures for the resistance of the invaders, continually and repeatedly urging upon it, however, the necessity for prompt and decisive action. He also continued to maintain that all the misfortunes of the country came from that fatal mismanagement to which the Chamber had been compelled to submit; and, after the disastrous battles near Metz and the approach of the Crown Prince at the head of his army towards the capital, endeavored to inspire his countrymen with patriotic zeal, denouncing as thrice accursed the citizen of France who founded his hopes for the future upon defeat and ruin.

Such has been the career of Jules Favre—a career which is happily as free from fanaticism as it is from treachery to the cause of liberty and justice. He has never displayed any tendencies towards the "irreconcilable" school of which Raspail and Rochefort are the types, and thus retains the confidence and respect of those who preferred stability under a Bonaparte to anarchy under a modern Jacobin. In patriotism, in experience, in discretion, in ability, and in devotion to the cause of true Republicanism, Jules Favre is the foremost man in France. He combines perhaps in a greater degree than any of his contemporaries the elements of stability and radicalism; and, if a republic is to rise from the ruins of the empire, his claims upon the chief magistracy of the nation are superior to those of any who may antagonize them. Whether, in the tumult of the great upheaval, his rare worth will receive its fitting recognition is a question which time alone can decide.

THE REVOLUTION IN PARIS.

CORRECTED LIST OF THE NATIONAL DEFENSE GOVERNMENT—THE NEW MINISTRY.

PARIS, September 5.—The following is a corrected list of the Provision Government taking the name of the National Defense Government:—Emmanuel Arago, Cremieux, Jules Favre, Jules Ferry, Gambetta, Garnier-Pages, Glais-Bizoin, Pelletan, Ernest Picard, Rochefort, Jules Simon. The Ministry is as follows:

Minister of Foreign Affairs—Jules Favre.
Minister of Justice—Isaac Cremieux.
Minister of the Interior—Leon Gambetta.
Minister of Finance—Ernest Picard.

Superintendent of Public Works—Pierre Dorian.

Minister of Commerce—Joseph Magnin.

Superintendent of Public Instruction—Jules Simon.

Minister of Marine—Martin Fourichon.

Minister of War—Louis Jules Trochu; also, President of the Committee.

The French Republic of 1870 has been recognized by the United States, and this comes about by the fall of Napoleon.

THE DECISIVE BATTLE OF THE WAR.

MARSHAL MACMAHON'S WHOLE ARMY CAPTURED—THE EMPEROR SURRENDERS TO KING WILLIAM—MACMAHON SEVERELY WOUNDED—DESPATCH FROM KING WILLIAM.

BEFORE SEDAN, FRANCE,
Friday, Sept. 2—1:22 P. M.

From the King to the Queen.—A capitulation, whereby the whole army at Sedan are prisoners of war, has just been concluded with Gen. Wimpfen, commanding, instead of Marshal MacMahon, who is wounded. The Emperor surrendered himself to me, as he has no command, and left everything to the Regency at Paris. His residence I shall appoint after an interview with him at a rendezvous to be fixed immediately. Under God's guidance, what a course events have taken!

THE BATTLE AND THE SURRENDER.

THE FRENCH CUT OFF FROM MEZIERES—SEDAN COMPLETELY SURROUNDED—THE FORTIFICATIONS CARRIED BY THE BAVARIANS—THE EMPEROR'S LETTER TO KING WILLIAM.

(The following account I take from the New York *Tribune's* correspondent. This paper, during the war, had full and correct accounts of every battle, and its dispatches were copied throughout the United States.—ED.)

"The battle of Sedan began at 6 A. M. on the 1st of September. Two Prussian corps were in position on the west of Sedan, having got there by a long forced march, so as to cut off the French retreat to Mézières. On the south of Sedan was the First Bavarian Corps, and on the east, across the Meuse, the Second Bavarian Corps. The Saxons were on the northeast with the Guards. I was with the King throughout the day on the hill above the Meuse, commanding a splendid view of the valley of the river and the field.

"After a tremendous battle, the Prussians having completely surrounded Sedan, and the Bavarians having actually entered the fortifications of the city, the Emperor capitulated at 5:15 P. M. His letter to the king of Prussia said:

"'As I cannot die at the head of my army, I lay my sword at the feet of your Majesty.'

"Napoleon left Sedan for the Prussian head-quarters at Vendresse, at 7 A. M. on the 2d September. MacMahon's whole army comprising 100,000 men, capitulated without conditions. The Prussians had 240,000 troops engaged or in reserve, the French 120,000."

Head-quarters King of Germans, eight miles from Sedan, Thursday night Sept. 1, 1870.

WHAT THE FRENCH PRISONERS SAY.

After their defeats on the 30th and 31st ult., the French retreated *en masse* on Sedan. and encamped around it. From what I learned from the French prisoners—of whom, as you may imagine, there was no lack in our quarter—it seems that they fully believed that the road to Mézières would always be open to them, and that therefore, in case of another defeat before Sedan, their retreat would be easily accomplished.

A FORCED MARCH.

On the evening of Wednesday, from 5 to 8 o'clock, I was at the Crown Prince's quarters at Chemery, a village some thirteen miles from Sedan to the south-south-west on the main road. At half-past five we saw that there was a great movement among the troops encamped all around us, and we thought at first that the King was riding through the bivouacs; but soon the 37th regiment came pouring through the village, their band playing *Die Wacht am Rhein* as they marched along with a swinging stride. I saw at once by the men's faces that something extraordinary was going on. It was soon plain that the troops were in the lightest possible marching order. All their knapsacks were left behind, and they were carrying nothing but cloaks slung around their shoulders, except that one or two *bon vivants* had retained their camp-kettles. But if the camp-kettles were left behind, the cartouche-cases were there—hanging heavily in front of the men's belts, unbalanced, as they ought to be, by the knapsacks. Soon I learned that the whole Prussian corps—those lent from Prince Frederick Charles' army, the Second Army, and the Crown Prince's—were making a forced march to the left in the direction of Donchery and Mézières, in order to shut in MacMahon's army in the west, and so drive them against the Belgian frontier. I learned from the officers of the Crown Prince's staff that at the same time, while we were watching regiment after regiment pass through Chemery the Saxons and the Guards, 80,000 strong on the Prussian right, under Prince Albert of Saxony, were also marching rapidly, to close on the doomed French army on the right bank of the Meuse, which they had crossed at Remilly, on Tuesday the 30th, in the direction of La Chapelle, a small village of 930 inhabitants on the road from Sedan to Bouillon, in Belgium, and the last village before crossing the frontier.

Anything more splendid than the men's marching, it would be impossible to imagine. I saw men lame in both feet hobbling along in the ranks, kind comrades less footsore carrying their needle-guns. Those who were actually incapable of putting one foot before another, had pressed peasants' wagons and every available conveyance into service, and were following in the rear, so as to be ready for the great battle, which all felt sure would come off on the morrow. The Bavarians, who, it is generally believed, do not march so well as they fight, were in the center, between us at Chemery and Sedan, encamped around the woods of La Marfee, famous for a great battle in 1641, during the wars of the League. When I had seen the last regiment dash through—for the pace at which they went can really not be called "marching" in the ordinary sense—I rode off about a quarter past eight in the evening for Vendresse where the King's headquarters were, and where I hoped to find house-room for man and beast, especially the latter, as being far the most important on the eve of a great battle.

When I got within about half a mile of Vendresse, going at a steady trot, a sharp "Halt!" rang out through the clear air. I brought my horse to a stand-still, knowing that Prussian sentries are not to be trifled with. As I pulled up 20 yards off, I heard the clicks of their locks as they brought their weapons to full cock and covered me. My reply being satisfactory, I jogged on into Vendresse, and my mare and myself had soon forgotten sentinels, forced marches, and coming battles, one of us on the straw, the other on the floor.

THE START FOR THE BATTLE-FIELD.

At seven, Thursday morning, my servant came to wake me, saying that the King's horses were harnessing, and that His Majesty would leave in half an hour for the battle-field; and as a cannonade had already been heard near Sedan, I jumped up, seized crusts of bread, wine, cigars, etc., and crammed them into my holster, taking my breakfast on the way.

Just as I got to my horse, King William drove out in an open carriage with four horses, for Chevange, about three and a half miles south of Sedan. Much against my will, I was compelled to allow the King's staff to precede me on the road to the scene of action, where I arrived myself soon after nine o'clock. It was impossible to ride fast, all the roads being blocked up with artillery, ammunition wagons, ambulances, etc. As I rode on to the crest of the hill which rises sharply about 600 or 700 feet above the little hamlet of Chevange, nestled in a grove below,

A MOST GLORIOUS PANORAMA.

burst on my view. As General Forsyth of the United States army remarked to me later in the day, it would have been worth the coming, merely to see so splendid a scene, without "battle's magnificently stern array." In the lovely valley below us, from the knoll on which I stood with the King and his staff, we could see not only the whole Valley of the Meuse (or Maas, as the Germans love to call the river that Louis XIV stole from them), but also beyond the great woods of Bois de Loup and Francheval into Belgium, and as far as the hilly forest of Numo on the other side of the frontier. Right at our feet lay the little town of Sedan, famous for its fortifications by Vauban, and as the birth-place of Turenne—the great Marshal. It is known, also, as the place where Sedan chairs originated. As we were only about two and a quarter miles from the town, we could easily distinguish its principal edifices without the aid of our field-glasses. On the left was a pretty church, its Gothic spire of sandstone offering a conspicuous target for the Prussian guns, had Gen. Moltke thought fit to bombard the town. To the right, on the southeast of the church, was a large barrack, with the fortifications of the citadel. Behind it and beyond this to the southeast again was the old chateau of Sedan, with picturesque, round-turreted towers of the sixteenth century, very useless even against four-pounder Krupp field-pieces. This building, I believe, is now an arsenal. Beyond this was the citadel—the heart of Sedan—on a rising hill above the Meuse to the southeast, but completely commanded by the hills on both sides the river which runs in front of the citadel.

A GRAVE FRENCH BLUNDER.

The French had flooded the low meadows in the valley before coming to the railway bridge at Bazeille, in order to stop the Germans from advancing on the town in that direction. With their usual stupidity (for one can find no other word for it), the French had failed to mine the bridge at Bazeille, and it was of immense service to the Prussians throughout the battle. The Prussians actually threw up earthworks on the iron bridge itself to protect it from the French, who more than once attempted early in the day to storm the bridge, in the hope of breaking the Bavarian communication between the right and left banks of the Meuse. This they were unable to do; and although their cannon-shot have almost demolished the parapet, the bridge itself was never materially damaged.

POSITION OF THE CONTENDING FORCES.

On the projecting spurs of the hill, crowned by the woods of La Marfee, of which I have already spoken, the Bavarians had posted two batteries of six-pounder rifled breech-loading steel Krupp guns, which kept up a duello till the very end of the day with the siege guns of Sedan across the Meuse. Still further to the right flank, or rather, to the east (for our line was a circular one—a cresent at first, with Sedan on the center like the star on the Turkish standard), was an undulating plain above the village of Bazeille. Terminating about a mile and a half from Sedan, at the woods near Rubecourt, midway—that is to say, in a line from Bazeille north—there is a ravine watered by a tiny brook, which was the scene of the most desperate struggle and of the most frightful slaughter of the whole battle. This stream, whose name I have forgotten, if it ever had one, runs right behind the town of Sedan.

From the woods of Fleigreuse on the north behind the town, rises a hill dotted with cottages and fruit-laden orchards, and crowned by the wood of La Garenne which runs down to the valley of which I have just spoken. Between this wood and the town were several French camps, their white shelter tents standing out clear among the dark fruit-trees. In these camps one could see throughout the day huge masses of troops which were never used. Even during the height of the battle, they stood as idle as Fitz John Porter's at the second battle of Bull-Run. We imagined that they must have been undisciplined Gardes Mobiles whom the French Generals dared not bring out against their enemy.

To the Prussian left of these French camps, separated from them by a wooded ravine, was a long bare hill, something like one of the hills on Long Island. This hill, on which was some of the hardest fighting of the day, formed one of the keys of the position of the French army. When once its crests were covered with Prussian artillery, the whole town of Sedan was completely at the mercy of the German guns, as they were not only above the town, but the town was almost within musket range of them.

Still further to the left lay the village of Illy, set on fire early in the day by the French shells. South of this the broken railway bridge, blown up by the French to protect their right, was a conspicuous object.

Right above the railway bridge on the line to Mézières was the wooded hill crowded by the new and most hideous "chateau," as he calls it, of one Monsieur Pave. It was here the Crown Prince and his staff stood during the day, having a rather more extensive but less central view, and therefore less desirable than ours, where stood the King, Count Bismarck, Von Roon, the War Minister, Gen. Moltke, and Gens. Sheridan and Forsyth—to say nothing of your correspondent.

THE PRUSSIAN PLAN OF BATTLE.

Having thus endeavored to give some faint idea of the scene of what is in all probability the decisive battle of the war, I will next give an account of the position of the different corps at the commencement of the action, premising that all the movements were of the simplest possible nature, the object of the Prussian generals being merely to close the crescent of troops with which they began into a circle by effecting a junction between the Saxon corps on their right and the Prussian corps on their left. This junction took place about noon, near the little village of Olley, on the Bazeille ravine, behind Sedan, of which I have already spoken. Once their terrible circle formed and well soldered together, it grew steadily smaller and smaller,

until at last the fortifications of Sedan itself were entered.

On the extreme right were the Saxons— one corps d'armee, with King William's Guards; also, a corps d'armee in reserve behind them. The Guards had suffered terribly at Gravelotte, where they met the Imperial Guard; and the King would not allow them to be again so cruelly decimated. Justice compels me to state that this arrangement was very far, indeed, from being pleasing to the Guards themselves, who are ever anxious to be in the forefront of the battle.

The Guards and Saxons, then about 75,000 strong, were all day on the right bank of the Meuse, between Rubecourt and La Chapelle, at which latter village Prince Albert of Saxony, who was in command of the two corps which have been formed into a little extra army by themselves, passed the night of Thursday.

The ground from Rubecourt to the Meuse was occupied by the First Bavarian Corps. The Second Bavarian Corps extended their front from near the Bazeille railway-bridge to a point on the high road from Donchery to Sedan, not far from the little village of Torcy. Below the hill on which the Crown Prince was placed, the ground from Torcy to Illy, through the large village of Floing, was held by the First and Third Prussian Corps, belonging to the army of Prince Frederick Charles, and temporarily attached to the army of the Crown Prince.

This was the position of the troops about 9 o'clock on Thursday morning, September 1st, and no great advance took place till later than that, for the artillery had at first all the work to do. Still further to the left, near Donchery, there were 20,000 Würtembergers ready to cut off the French from Mézières, in case of their making a push for that fortress.

THE FORCES ENGAGED.

The number of the Prussian troops engaged was estimated by General Moltke at 240,000, and that of the French at 120,000. We know that MacMahon had with him on Tuesday 120,000 men, that is, four corps, his own, that lately commanded by General De Failly, now under General Le Brun; that of Felix Douay, brother of General Abel Douay, killed at Weissenburg; and a fourth corps principally composed of Garde Mobile, the name of whose commander has escaped me. MacMahon, although wounded, commanded in chief on the French side.

It is almost needless to say that the real Commander-in-Chief of the Prussians was Von Moltke; with the Crown Prince and Prince Albert of Saxony immediately next in command.

OPENING OF THE BATTLE.

There were a few stray cannon shots fired, merely to obtain the range, as soon as it was

CITIZENS AND SOLDIERS AT WORK ON THE FORTIFICATIONS
OF PARIS.

Bürger und Soldaten arbeiten an den Verschanzungen von Paris.

PRINCE LEOPOLD OF HOHENZOLLERN-SIGMARINGEN.
Prinz Leopold von Hohenzollern-Sigmaringen.

light; but the real battle did not begin until 6 o'clock, becoming a sharp artillery fight at 9, when the batteries had each got within easy range, and the shells began to do serious mischief. At 11:55 the musketry fire in the valley behind Sedan, which had opened about 11:25, became exceedingly lively—being one continuous rattle, only broken by the loud growling of the mitrailleuses, which played with deadly effect upon the Saxon and Bavarian columns. Gen. Sheridan, by whose side I was standing at the time, told me that he did not remember ever to have heard such a well-sustained fire of small arms. It made itself heard above the roar of the batteries at our feet.

At 12 o'clock precisely the Prussian battery of six guns on the slope above the broken railway bridge over the Meuse, near La Villette, had silenced two batteries of French guns at the foot of the bare hill already mentioned, near the village of Floing. At 12:10 the French infantry, no longer supported by their artillery, were compelled to retire to Floing, and soon afterward the junction between the Saxons and Prussians behind Sedan was announced to us by Gen. Von Roon, eagerly peering through a large telescope, as being safely completed.

THE FRENCH SURROUNDED.

From this moment the result of the battle could no longer be doubtful. The French were completely surrounded and brought to bay. At 12:25 we were all astonished to see clouds of retreating French infantry on the hill between Floing and Sedan, a Prussian battery in front of St. Menges making accurate practice with percussion shells among the receding ranks. The whole hill for a quarter of an hour was literally covered with Frenchmen running rapidly.

Less than half an hour afterward—at 12:50—Gen. Von Roon called our attention to another French column in full retreat to the right of Sedan, on the road leading from Bazeille to the La Garenne wood. They never halted until they came to a red-roofed house on the outskirts of Sedan itself. Almost at the same moment Gen. Sheridan, who was using my opera-glass, asked me to look at a third French column moving up a broad, grass-covered road through the La Garenne wood, immediately above Sedan, doubtless to support the troops defending the important Bazeille ravine to the northeast of the town.

THE KEY OF THE POSITION.

At 1 o'clock the French batteries on the edge of the wood toward Torcy and above it opened a vigorous fire on the advancing Prussian columns of the Third Corps, whose evident intention it was to storm the hill northwest of La Garenne, and so gain the key of the position on that side. At 1:05 yet another French battery near the wood opened on the Prussian columns, which

were compelled to keep shifting their ground till ready for their final rush at the hills, in order to avoid offering so good a mark to the French shells. Shortly afterward we saw the first Prussian skirmishers on the crest of the La Garenne hills above Torcy. They did not seem to be in strength, and General Sheridan, standing behind me, exclaimed:

"Ah! the beggars are too weak; they can never hold that position against all those French."

The General's prophecy soon proved correct, for the French advanced at least six to one; and the Prussians were forced to retreat down the hill to seek re-enforcements from the columns which were hurrying to their support. In five minutes they came back again, this time in greater force, but still terribly inferior to those huge French masses.

AN UNSUCCESSFUL CAVALRY CHARGE.

"Good heavens! The French cuirassiers are going to charge them," cried General Sheridan; and sure enough, the regiment of cuirassiers, their helmets and breast-plates flashing in the September sun, formed in sections of squadrons and dashed down on the scattered Prussian skirmishers, without deigning to form a line. Squares are never used by the Prussians, and the infantry received the cuirassiers with a crushing "quick-fire," *schnellfeuer*, at about a hundred yards distance, loading and firing with extreme rapidity, and shooting with unfailing precision into the dense French squadrons. The effect was startling. Over went horses and men in numbers, in masses, in hundreds; and the regiment of proud French cuirassiers went hurriedly back in disorder; went back faster than it came; went back scarcely a regiment in strength, and not at all a regiment in form. Its comely array was suddenly changed into shapeless and helpless crowds of flying men.

CAVALRY PURSUED BY INFANTRY.

The moment the cuirassiers turned back, the brave Prussians actually dashed forward in hot pursuit at double-quick; infantry evidently pursuing flying cavalry. Such a thing has not often been recorded in the annals of war. I know not when an example to compare precisely with this has occurred. There was no more striking episode in the battle.

"There will be a devil of a fight for that crest before it is won or lost," said Sheridan, straining his eyes through his field-glass at the hill which was not three miles from us. The full sun was shining upon that hill; we gazing upon it had the sun behind us.

ANOTHER FRUITLESS CAVALRY CHARGE.

At 1:30 French cavalry—this time, I presume, a regiment of *carabiniers*—made another dash at the Prussians, who, on their part, were receiving reinforcements every moment; but the *carabiniers* met with the same fate as their brethren in iron jackets, and were sent to the right about with heavy loss. The Prussians took advantage of their flight to advance their line about 200 yards nearer the line which the French infantry held.

ANOTHER FRENCH BLUNDER.

This body of adventurous Prussians split into two portions, the two parts leaving a break of a hundred yards in their line. We were not long in perceiving the object of this movement, for the little white puffs from the crest behind the skirmishers, followed by a commotion in the dense French masses, show us that these "*diables de Prussiens*" have contrived, heaven only knows how, to get two four-pounders up the steep ground, and have opened fire on the French. Something must at this point have been very much mismanaged with the French infantry; for, instead of attacking the Prussians. whom they still outnumbered by at least two to one, they remained in column on the hill, and though seeing their only hope of retrieving the day vanishing from before their eyes, still they did not stir. Then the French cavalry tried to do

A LITTLE BALAKLAVA BUSINESS,

tried, but without the success of the immortal six hundred, who took the guns on which they charged. The cuirassiers came down once more, this time riding straight for the two field-pieces; but before they came within 200 yards of the guns, the Prussians formed line as if on parade, and waiting till those furious French horsemen had ridden to a point not fifty yards away, they fired. The volley seemed to us to empty the saddles of almost the whole of the leading squadron. The dead so strewed the ground as to block the path of the squadron following, and close before them the direct and dangerous road they had meant to follow. Their dash at the guns became a halt.

RETREAT OF THE FRENCH.

When once this last effort of the French horse had been made and had failed—failed, though pushed gallantly so far as men and horses could go—the French infantry fell swiftly back toward Sedan. It fell back because it saw that the chance of its carrying that fiercely-contested hill was gone, and saw also that the Prussians holding the hill were crowning it with guns, so that their own line could not much longer be held facing it. In an instant, as the French retired, the whole slope of the ground was covered by swarms of Prussian tirailleurs, who seemed to rise out of the ground, and push forward by help of every slight roughness or depression in the surface of the hill. As fast as the French went back these active enemies followed. After the last desperate charge of the French cavalry, General Sheridan remarked to me that he never saw any-

thing so reckless, so utterly foolish, as that last charge. " It was sheer murder."

The Prussians, after the French infantry fell back, advanced rapidly—so rapidly that the retreating squadrons of French cavalry, being too closely pressed, turned suddenly round and charged desperately once again. But it was all no use. The days of breaking squares are over. The thin blue line soon stopped the Gallic onset.

It struck me as most extraordinary, that at this point the French had

NEITHER ARTILLERY NOR MITRAILLEUSES,

especially the latter, on the field to cover their infantry. The position was a most important one and certainly worth straining every nerve to defend. One thing was clear enough, that the French infantry, after once meeting the Prussians, declined to try conclusions with them again, and that the cavalry were seeking to encourage them by their example. About 2 o'clock still other reinforcements came to the Prussians over this long-disputed hill between Torcy and Sedan to support the regiments already established there.

HAVOC AMONG THE BAVARIANS.

At the time that this great conflict was going on under Fritz's eyes, another was fought not less severe and as murderous for the Bavarians as the one I have attempted to describe, was for the French. If there was a want of Mitrailleuses on the hill above Torcy, there was certainly no lack of them in the Bazeille ravine. On that side there was, for more than an hour, one continuous roar of musketry and mitrailleuses. Two Bavarian officers told me that the loss in their regiments was terrific, and that it was the mitrailleuses which made the havoc.

THE FRENCH FALL BACK ON SEDAN.

At 2:05 in the afternoon, the French totally abandoned the hill between Torcy and Sedan, and fell back on the faubourg of Caval, just outside the ramparts of the town. "Now the battle is lost for the French." said General Sheridan, to the delight of the Prussian officers. One would almost have imagined that the French had heard his words—they had hardly been uttered, when there came a lull in the firing all along the line, or rather circle; as such it had now become.

BELGIAN NEUTRALITY.

Count Bismarck chose that moment to come and have a talk with his English and American friends. I was anxious to know what the Federal Chancellor had done about the neutrality of Belgium, now threatened, and my curiosity was soon gratified. "I have told the Belgian Minister of War," said Count Bismarck, "that so long as the Belgian troops do their utmost to disarm any number of French soldiers who may cross

CROWN PRINCE FREDERICK WILLIAM,
Kronprinz Friedrich Wilhelm,

KING WILLIAM I.
König Wilhelm I.

the frontier, I will strictly respect the neutrality of Belgium; but if, on the contrary, the Belgians, either through negligence or inability, do not disarm and capture every man in French uniform who sets his foot in their country, we shall at once follow the enemy into neutral territory with our troops, considering that the French have been the first to violate the Belgian soil. I have been down to have a look at the Belgian troops near the frontier," added Count Bismarck, "and I confess they do not inspire me with a very high opinion of their martial ardor or discipline. When they have their great coats on, one can see a great deal of paletot, but hardly any soldier."

BISMARCK'S FIRST MISTAKE.

I asked his Excellency where he thought the Emperor was: "In Sedan?" "Oh, no!" was the reply: "Napoleon is not very wise, but he is not so foolish as to put himself in Sedan just now." For once in his life, Count Bismarck was wrong.

At 2:45 the King came to the place where I was standing. He remarked that he thought the French were about to try to break out just beneath us in front of the Second Bavarian Corps. At 3:50 General Sheridan told me that Napoleon and Louis were in Sedan.

BRAVERY OF THE BAVARIANS.

At 3:20 the Bavarians below us not only contrived to get themselves inside the fortifications of Sedan, but to maintain themselves here, working their way forward from house to house. About 4, there was a great fight for the possession of the ridge above Bazeille. That carried, Sedan was swept on all sides by the Prussian cannon. This point of vantage was carried at 4:40. When carried, there could no longer be a shade of doubt as to the ultimate fate of Sedan.

A RETROSPECTION.

THE FINAL BLOW AT SEDAN.

The general headquarters of the army of the Crown Prince, and probably the bulk of his force, advanced no further than Bar-le-Duc, but Frederick William himself is reported to have slept at Chalons on the night of August 27, his advance being then at a point about ten miles further west, and eighty miles from Paris. But at that time the movement of MacMahon towards Mézières was fully developed, and the army of the Crown Prince was turned to the right to follow him up, while the detached portion of the Prussian army around Metz was pushed towards the northwest to intercept the French advance. As soon as MacMahon had collected his forces in the neighborhood of Rethel, he began a movement directly east towards Montmedy, and daily conflicts between detached portions of the hostile armies occurred, with almost unvarying success on the Prussian side. By the 30th of August, the whole French army was fairly in motion

in the direction of Montmedy, and on tha day there was a fierce encounter with the Prussians at Beaumont, about fourteen miles west of Montmedy, in which the corps of General de Failly was severely handled. The French were driven to the northwest upon Sedan, where the conflict became general on the 31st of August, and continued into the 1st of September. On the last day of August, it would seem that the Prussians suffered severely, but when the final struggle came on Thursday, the 1st of September, they mustered 240,000 men, while MacMahon had at the outside not more than 120,000. Although severely wounded, he still retained the chief command, the German forces being under the immediate direction of General von Moltke, with the Crown Prince Frederick William of Prussia, and the Crown Prince Albert of Saxony next in command. The corps of the Prussian commander were posted to the left, those of the Saxon to the right of the French position. The plan of attack was to effect a junction between the two, and thereby enclose the enemy in a semi-circle. This object was fully accomplished by noon, and by 3 o'clock the battle had been transformed into a rout, with the French in full flight.

THE CAPITULATION OF MACMAHON.

Darkness put an end to the pursuit, and on the ensuing day, September 2, the Prussians prepared to assault Sedan, by which the French retreat was protected. But it was not necessary. At noon, General Wimpffen, who had succeeded the disabled hero of Magenta in command, left Sedan with a flag of truce, and at half-past 1 o'clock the fortress and the remnants of MacMahon's army were formally and unconditionally surrendered. When MacMahon went into the engagement on the morning of September 1st, he had under his command, as already stated, about 120,000 men. The number who were placed *hors de combat* during the fight it is impossible as yet to ascertain, and it is equally impossible to estimate with accuracy the number that became prisoners of war through the ceremony of capitulation. The *Independance Belge* of Brussels places the number of French in Sedan at the time of its capitulation at 70,660, and states that on the 4th, 15,000 more surrendered, while 30,000 took refuge upon the neutral soil of Belgium. But this much is certain, that the victory of Sedan, followed, as it was, by the capitulation of the entire French army, was one of the most brilliant on record. After all was over, the Crown Prince resumed his triumphant march on Paris.

THE SURRENDER OF NAPOLEON.

But it was accompanied by a circumstance which imparted to it additional lustre and importance. The Emperor Napoleon, after the vicissitudes narrated by us yesterday, had arrived at Sedan on the 27th of August. According to some reports, the Prince Imperial had preceded him thither, while others state that he made his escape into Belgium. General Wimpffen bore with him a letter to King William from the Emperor, of which two or three versions have been published, the Paris *Gaulois* giving the following as its exact text:—

"Having no command in the army, and having placed all my authority in the hands of the Empress as regent, I herewith surrender my sword to the King of Prussia."

While, according to other reports, the document ran thus:—

"As I cannot die at the head of my army, I lay my sword at the feet of your Majesty."

But he surrendered, and at an interview with King William, who had accompanied the army of the Crown Prince in its march to the north from the neighborhood of Barle-Duc, held immediately after the capitulation of MacMahon's army, Wilhelmshof, near Cassel, was assigned as the place of his residence for the time being. He started without delay on his journey thither, by way of Liege, through Belgium, accompanied by a suite of one hundred persons, and an armed Prussian escort. The Prince Imperial is on the way to join him, if he was not with him at the time of his surrender, and the presence of the ex-Empress will soon render the fallen Imperial family complete.

Meanwhile Paris, which for nearly nineteen years had been awed into subjection by the terror of his bayonets and the inspiration of his name, is revelling in shouts of "Vive la Republique!" and the only semblance of French authority in France is the Provisional Republic, which Favre, Gambetta, and Trochu have set up on the ruins of the Bonaparte throne.

Such is the history of the conflict which General Prim precipitated upon Europe by proposing Prince Leopold of Hohenzollern-Sigmaringen, as a candidate for the throne of Spain. The ex-Emperor—we have already become used to the expressive prefix—resented the scheme of Prim ostensibly "as a check and a menace to France," in reality as a defiance of his well-known hostility to what he had been pleased to term the aggrandizing spirit of Prussia. He sought to throw the entire responsibility for it upon the Prussian King; and, not content with its abandonment, demanded a guarantee that no Prussian Prince would ever be suffered to ascend the throne of Charles V. This humiliating demand was rejected, and Napoleon declared that he would enforce it at the point of the sword. On the 28th of July, he affixed the magical name of Napoleon to a proclamation in which he assumed the chief command of an army of half a million of soldiers, whom he proposed forthwith to lead on a triumphant march upon Berlin. On the 2d of September, only five weeks afterwards, he laid his sword at the feet of King William, and surrendered himself a prisoner of war.

Thus ends the story of the Third Napoleon and the Second Empire. Unhappily the tribulations which they have bequeathed to France are, perchance, but just begun.

THINGS IN AND AROUND PARIS.

TREACHERY IN HIGH PLACES.

You may like to know what is considered in Paris, by those best informed, to be the truth in relation to the stories with which the air is full concerning the treachery in high places that has been practised in, France. It was understood, sometime ago, that Marshal Lebœuf had completely deceived the Emperor and the Corps Legislatif in regard to the readiness of the country for war. "We are ready," he had said, "and by 'ready' I mean that if the war were to last a year we should not have to buy as much as a button for a gaiter." This was bad enough; but it now appears that the wife of the Marshal, who is a Prussian, obtained from her husband the full particulars of the plan of military operations which had been decided upon, and then found means to communicate this invaluable information to Bismarck, and through him to Von Moltke. Thus, when the game of war began, the Prussians were in the condition of a player who knew all the cards in his opponent's hand and exactly how he intended to play them. That success should follow an advantage so great as this, was only what was to be expected. This, however, is not all. The *Gaulois* has made public what was whispered about Paris all last week—namely, that a mysterious prisoner was incarcerated at Vincennes, whose identity was so carefully concealed that the ordinary wardens of the fort were not allowed to see him. Opinion is divided as to whether this reproduction of the man in the iron mask is Lebœuf, Rochefort, or the author of the false news published on the Bourse three weeks ago, and no Joseph or Daniel has arisen to interpret the mystery. But some arrests have been made of female spies, of whose identity there is no doubt. The first was no less a personage than Madame la Comtesse de Behague—"the luxurious syren who boasted of having the King of Prussia, the Prince, and the Grand Duke of Baden at her feet."

ANOTHER SPY STORY.

In a Strasbourg hotel some Algerian tirailleurs, officers, sous officers, and privates were at breakfast, the first they had eaten in peace for a week. An intruder came in with many bows and begged permission to place himself at table, offering to pay his share. "You don't know me, but I am not quite a stranger to the great army family. Captain Brunet, Twenty-one of the line, is known to some of you, I dare say. He is my very dearest friend, almost my brother."

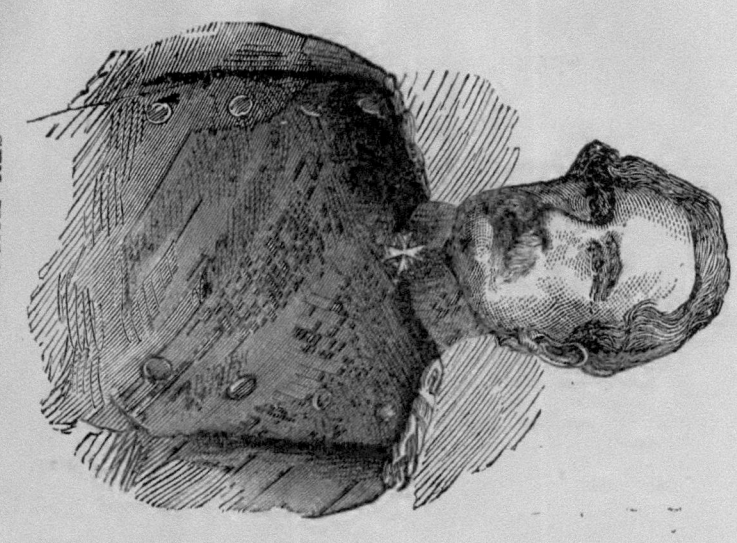

GEN. VON STEINMETZ.
General von Steinmetz.

PRINCE ROYAL FREDERICK CHARLES,
Prinz Friedrich Karl.

Nobody knew Captain Brunet, but his name was a passport among soldiers. The stranger took his cotelette, and was chatting easily with his companions when an officer of the Twenty-first came in: "Parbleu! here is the very man to tell you all about your friend. Lieutenant, allow us to present a friend of one of yours; you know Captain Brunet?" "What Brunet?" "Brunet of the Twenty-first." "No such man in our regiment since I joined it ten years ago." The stranger is confused. His lively tone is changed. Some Turcos asked the lieutenant: "Are you sure there was no such man as Captain Brunet?" "Just as sure as that you are standing there." "Why, then, he must be——," and they began to close round the stranger. "Monsieur is in my company," said the captain of tirailleurs, a solid man. "Go on with your breakfast, sir; shall I hand you the cheese? Take some of this conserve." Coffee and *chasse*—breakfast was over. The big tirailleur called for the bill and paid. Taking the stranger's arm, he walked outside on to the sidewalk, drew his revolver, and blew out the spy's brains

THE FATE OF SPIES IN WAR.
[From the Jewish Leader.]

It is a deplorable fact that a good number of spies have up to this moment been employed in the war which is now being carried on between the two great European Powers. Those who carry out this treacherous system are severely punished when caught, for what is a spy else than a secret assassin, owing to whose paid treason large masses of soldiers often perish, whereas they might have preserved their lives in honest, open combat?

If we read in the Scripture of spies, the mission with which they were entrusted is not, by any means, comparable or analogous with the functions performed by the treacherous individuals of our times, above referred to. Yet it has been recorded that these spies were disagreeable to Moses, and he only consented to send out spies in order to tranquilize the turbulent and refractory people as to the condition of the country. Moses cannot have cared about the reports which these spies would bring him, as his trust in God must have rendered them a matter of indifference to him.

The aim and object of Joshua in sending out the two spies to Jericho was equally to reanimate and encourage the dismayed hearts of Israel by favorable intelligence (thus we understand the comment of Kimchi). Also, the missions of the messengers to Ai (Joshua 7) was only for the purpose of tranquillizing the people about the selection of no more than three thousand warriors for the expedition against that city. That this expedition miscarried proves that it was not the intention of Joshua to gather such information as could be favorable to him.

The two messengers whom David sent out to seek Saul (1 Samuel xxvi. 5) were no spies of whom David availed himself in order to do any harm to King Saul. In like manner the Meraglim of Absalom (2 Samuel xv. 10) were nothing but messengers to the different tribes. Even the messengers of the tribe of Dan to the house of Micah were not sent out as spies.

FRENCH MILITARY VANITY.

The French papers call the attention of the military authorities to the excellent system adopted by the enemy in its reconnoissances, and say that while French commanders are nearly always taken by surprise, the Prussians are perfectly well-informed of the whereabouts of their adversaries. This is, in a great degree, owing to the vanity of the French officers, who think that they can afford to despise all information and every suggestion not coming from one of themselves. Before Woerth, a captain on outpost duty was warned by the peasants that a body of Uhlans were cutting the telegraph wires and destroying the railroad. His only answer was: What's that to me—*Qu'est ce que ca me fait*—we are not fighting with the telegraph, are we?

It is very different on the other side; there no piece of information is disregarded, and a detachment at once proceeds to investigate the truth of every report. The reconnoissances are made by small bodies of picked horsemen under the command of a chief of intelligence, who can always find among his troopers some one who has been born near the frontier, or whose trade previous to the war had brought him into relations with the country and its inhabitants. With such a guide it is impossible to make mistakes, and as each scout is furnished with a colored print of the various uniforms in the French army, he is able to inform the authorities exactly what they wish to know.

"THE SOLDIER'S PIPE."
"RESPECTFULLY DEDICATED TO SMOKERS."

It would be unjust, considering all the abuse levelled at tobacco-smokers, and how often they are solemnly told that tobacco destroys all their energies, not to admit that the success of the Germans in the present war is rather a feather in the smoker's cap. These misguided men seem to live on tobacco; The Uhlans, who in little parties of three or four trot gaily in advance and take possession of fortified towns, invariably carry pipes in their mouths. The Mayor of each town is directed to find cigars for everybody before anything else is done. The German troops, it is stated, think but little of a scarcity of provisions—they fight as well without their dinner as with it—but tobacco is indispensable to them. On the whole, we fear experience shows that a smoking army is capable of greater endurance and of making greater efforts than a non-smoking army. The gun without the pipe would be of little avail, nor can we be much surprised at this when we reflect that the quantity of foul air we are called upon to inhale in this world is probably far more injurious to health than the tobacco smoke, which, although it acts as an antidote to the poison of the atmosphere, gets no thanks for its pains, but only reproachful language.

ENGLAND AND FRANCE.

M. LOUIS BLANC ON ENGLISH OPINION.

Writing to *Le Temps*, under date of August 23, M. Louis Blanc remarks: "In the critical circumstances in which we are placed it is necessary above all things that we should have courage to look on boldly into our position. To shut our eyes with indifference would be a crime. To be wanting in courage would be an opprobrium, but to nourish illusions would be almost an act of idiocy. In order to place ourselves in a position to meet danger, the first condition is to comprehend its extent. It would, indeed, be a strange transformation of the French nation if it had lost its heroic habit of adapting its energies to its perils. Those who might be disposed to veil the dangers in order to give heart to the nation, calumniate and outrage it. When we come to examine the picture of our position as it is presented by the more or less official journals which are published in Paris, in contrast with that presented by the English press, a fear is aroused lest France should be ignorant of how seriously she is menaced, and how important it is for her safety that she should again become her old self. The English do not know—and yet history exists to teach them—of what the great arm of France is capable, when they regard her condition as desperate. In the first place, nothing that bears an official French character obtains the slightest credence. Every telegram signed by the King of Prussia is accepted in England as an article of faith. Every telegram announcing that our army has gained a success is literally regarded as naught. When the conflicting doubts of the murderous battle of the 16th were received here, we read upon the placards of the newspapers: 'Great victory of the Prussians. The French claim a victory.' In other words, the Prussians had conquered because they said so. As to the French, the probability was, that they were lying. For a Frenchman living in England is not this heart-breaking? There is no one here that does not suppose that for Napoleon it is a question of life or death to conceal reverses which are the consequences of his imprudence, his incapacity, and his blind and foolish precipitation. There is no one who does not say: 'Every defeat sustained by those soldiers of France, whose almost superhuman intrepidity seemed to do violence to victory, is a formidable accusation directed against the Empire.'

"It is necessary, therefore, that the black side of things should be concealed at any cost. The safety of the Empire depends upon it, and the Emperor knows it. There lies in part the secret of the incredulity unfortunately only too intelligible against which are powerless the most formal assertions of the authorized depositaries of power in France. They would be believed if it could be imagined that they had no other anxiety than to save the country. They are not believed, because the anxiety to save the country is thought to be complicated with a desire to preserve the dynasty."

HIS VIEW.

Bismarck said, "We wish to retain the sympathy of the United States, and yet we find it gradually receding from us, now that France has been declared a Republic. It is but natural that a Republic so great as the United States of America should sympathize with a younger one, but do not the people of those United States make a mistake in their impetuosity to be on 'the right side?' We would wish to treat for peace, and with a proper representative for France would we do so, but we can never recognize a 'gutter Republic,' made up from the mob, and led by men whose ambitious aim is *distinction* and *lucrative positions*."

SONG OF THE GERMAN SOLDIERS IN ALSACE.

*Air.—"*ICH HATTE EINEN CAMERAD.*"*

In Alsace, over the Rhine,
There lives a Brother of mine;
  It grieves my soul to say
  He hath forgot the day
We were one land and line.

Dear Brother, torn apart,
Is 't true that changed thou art?
  The French have clapped on thee
  Red breeches, as we see;
Have they Frenchified thy heart?

Hark! that's the Prussian drum,
And it tells the time has come.
  We have made one "Germany,"
  One "Deutschland," firm and free
And our civil strifes are dumb.

Thee also, fighting sore,
Ankle-deep in German gore,
  We have won. Ah, Brother dear!
  Thou art German—dost thou hear?
They shall never part us more.

Who made this song of mine?
Two comrades by the Rhine;—
  A Suabian man began it,
  And a Pomeranian sang it,
In Alsace on the Rhine.

THE TERRIBLE UHLANS.

Capt. Jeannerod, the correspondent of *Le Temps*, writing from Mézières-Charleville, after the battles at Metz, of the conduct of the German troops, says that the reports of the Prussian doings are necessarily much exaggerated, but that isolated acts of violence have occurred, to which the alarm felt is in some degree traceable. Here is an incident which he relates illustrative of these exaggerations:

"A Prussian soldier was lying on the ground in a field; a doctor, near at hand, bandaged his wounds, and, having finished was about to mount his horse, when a Uhlan came up and shot him through the head with a pistol. Enormous as this seems it must be true, for everywhere I have heard the same story. One of my informants was an old dragoon of the Guard, one of the rare survivors of his regiment, which was annihilated in the battle of the 16th. 'We have been crushed,' he said, 'but each one of us had struck down three : and now, since they have fired upon the doctors, no more quarter! I met one this morning, lost in a wood. He had thrown away his gun, crying, 'Friend, friend!' 'No friend,' I replied, and ran my sword through his body.' Some Chasseurs d'Afrique have also declared in my presence 'No more quarter.' * * * Evidently the war between the two armies is assuming a character of fury and of extermination. * * * The Uhlan will deserve, after this war, to hold the same rank in the Prussian army as the Zouave does with us. 'The Uhlans are everywhere,' said a young peasant to me. Mounted upon excellent horses, four or five of them arrive in a village, and the whole canton knows that evening that the Prussians have arrived, though the *corps d'armée* may be 15 kilometres off. But that is unknown ; and hence the dread of firing upon these four or five Uhlans, lest, for a single enemy thus dispatched, a whole commune might be put to fire and sword. So much for the terror produced by Prussian arms ; but they also know how to caress the people. In the environs of Metz, nothing is spoken of but the Prussian organization, and the facility with which it adapts itself, for the moment, to the local customs of the country that is invaded. They have even gone so far as to promise to the employés of the Sarreguemines Railroad to maintain them on their present footing, though this is very superior to the condition of similar employés in Rhenish Prussia. In the towns, small and large, wherever their conduct will be talked of, the same dexterous handling is shown. Half from policy, half from natural inclination, the conduct of the enemy in certain localities has left nothing to be complained of. As against the villages burnt on the hills of Gravelotte, other cases are cited where the inhabitants were quickly reassured. A young peasant girl said before me that it was very wrong to be frightened ; that the enemy had been very gentle and considerate, had taken nothing, but contented themselves with asking for what they wanted, and paying what was asked. And the peasant girl added one thing which was very sad, but which ought to be made known: 'Our own soldiers did a great deal more mischief.' "

THE PRINCESS ALICE AT HOME.

THE HOSPITAL AT DARMSTADT.

A correspondent of *The Pall Mall Gazette,* who visited the hospital for the wounded at Darmstadt, which is under the special charge of the Princess Alice, writes : " Certainly, nothing can be more admirably managed ;

and of those I have seen as yet it is the brightest, airiest, and most cheerful. The principal building is a permanent one of stone and glass—an ex-conservatory. It stands in charming gardens, with their flower-beds, and shrubberies, and fountains, which, as the Princess says, the Frenchmen gallantly tell her remind them of the water-works of Versailles. Through these are scattered a number of *succursales*—wooden pavilions where the double rows of beds stand at ample intervals, with canvas doors at the ends, to be looped up at will, and with openings in the roof, protected from the wet, but open to the wind. The Princess says the French strongly protest against the fresh air, while the Germans, on the contrary, very sensibly welcome it as the best of specifics. She ought to be mistress of the inward sentiments of the patients, for they all seem to take her into their inmost confidence. It was worth a journey from England alone to see the faces of the sufferers lighten up as they reflected the sisterly smiles on her. As she passed along and stopped and spoke to each, the invalid laid himself back on his pillow with an expression of absolute *bien être,* and for the moment seemed to find something more than an anodyne for his pain. Her passing along the wards applied the most infallible of tests to the cases. If her presence did not smooth the pain-wrinkles out of a man's face, or bring something like tranquillity to his drawn mouth, and cause a flash of light to his eye, you were quite sure to hear he was in an extremely bad way. Nor was it with the wounded alone she seemed the animating spirit of the place. Nurses and doctors and convalescents walking about all addressed her with the same cordial familiarity—only tempered by their evident reverence and love. The truth is, and one sees it everywhere else as in Darmstadt, this war has not merely made Germany a nation, but a family, and a thorough family feeling pervades North and South, high and low alike. Nothing seems regarded as a sacrifice, and the humblest work that can serve the great national cause is regarded as a pleasure and honor. The theatre at Mayence is given over to preparations for the hospital service, and the ladies of the place, old and young, go to work day and night in batches and in gangs, in the coarsest materials and roughest work. Here at Darmstadt no small portion of the Palace is devoted to the same purpose, and the work-rooms communicate directly with the Princess' apartments. There are piles of mattresses in the galleries, hills of blankets and cushions below, chests of lint, bundles of bandages, mountains of cushions, sandbags for absorbing blood, wooden receptacles for shattered limbs. There is a continual influx and constant outflow of all that. This afternoon the Princess' phaeton had the back seat piled high with cushions wanted for immediate use—decently covered up, it is true, with a carriage rug ; but there were so many of them that the rug was sheer hypocrisy and absurd illusion. A huge bundle of flannel seriously embarrassed the coachman's legs and style, while it says much for the paving of the Darmstadt streets that all the teapots stowed away in the sword case beneath the ladies' seat reached their destination in safety."

LIFE IN CAMP.

BEFORE METZ—HOW THE SOLDIERS LIVE—PREPARING A MEAL.

A correspondent of *The London Daily Telegraph* writes from the camp before Metz: The principal occupation, or rather the serious business of the day, in camp, is the preparation for a meal of some sort. Directly you wake, human nature at once requires some sustenance; you crave for a good hot cup of tea, especially if, as last night, you find yourself exposed to what Virgil calls a *placidus imber*. The fact was that the wall at the back of my shelter gave way, and I found myself lying with my head outside, the *gentle* rain falling plentifully on my head and face. The dry sticks which you have taken to bed with you to keep dry are produced as soon as day breaks, and a hot tin of coffee, without sugar or milk, helps to pull you together. The business of the day then commences. A rush is made for the nearest "Marketender" wagon that has come up from Gorze. In the following of almost every regiment there is attached to each company an individual called a "Marketender." Half soldier, half publican, and wholly thief, he is a curious mixture of cunning, courage, and dishonesty—terms, I am aware, that are strangely discordant, but which are all represented in the character of the Marketender.

His duty is, with his wagon, covered with canvas and drawn by two wretched-looking horses, to rob, plunder, or buy provisions at any of the villages he passes through, and to sell the produce to the soldiers of the particular company to which he is attached, the number of which is painted on his wagon and carried on his cap. Very often the Marketender has his better-half to help him—a virago, who out-brazens the sins of her husband, bullies the soldiers, and cringes to the officers. Mrs. Marketenderin is by no means an engaging-looking person. The one I have to do with wears a costume sufficiently ludicrous. A French soldier's cap covers her grizzled hair, the peak shading a face which, from exposure to the sun, looks like a piece of badly tanned leather; a Voltigeur's jacket envelops her body, and a large red bandanna is wound round her waist, where she carries a huge knife, with which to cut the hard, black bread into the pieces she dispenses to the soldiers; her arms and hands are brown-black, partly from exposure and partly from dirt, while, to complete her semi-military costume, the shortness of her petticoat reveals her feet incased

in a pair of long boots that have once been the property of some Prussian soldier, whose bones, in all probability, are now lying upon the plateau of Gorze. They both dispense their commodities in eager haste, and are not particular as to the change they give for a thaler. The appearance of the *vivandières* since the invasion of French territory has wonderfully improved, no doubt at the expense of *la belle France*, and the money they are making will, without doubt, enable them to eat their "Kartoffelsalat" and drink their "Zeltinger" for the rest of their days in peace and quietness on the banks of the Moselle, or wherever else they may please to settle down. If you are in favor, madame produces a piece of meat from the recesses of the wagon, and perhaps an onion, a piece of bread, and a glass of schnapps, for which you pay the moderate sum of one thaler. With these valuables you rush off to your shelter, wherever it may be, and, if the rain has not put your fire out, you improvise a meal, which, if not very *recherché*, at least fills your stomach. I was asked by the General to-day why I did not go and live in Gorze, like the other Englishmen? My answer was, simply, that I depended for information upon my own eyes, and not upon the retailed news of others. This seemed to amuse him vastly, and he patted me on the back, and answered, "Thank God! there are, then, some who will tell the truth as they see it, and not invent a parcel of lies." This was not very flattering to my brother correspondents. The band is really the luxury of the day. It plays in the afternoon, and the delicious airs of Beethoven, Mozart, and Meyerbeer transport one in imagination far from the surrounding scenes.

STRASBOURG AND PARIS.

A GERMAN MILITARY WRITER ON THEIR POWERS OF RESISTANCE.

The following extract from a letter of the well-known military writer, Julius Von Wickede, has a special interest in connection with the news from Strasbourg and Paris:

We are now besieging and bombarding Strasbourg and Metz, beyond all doubt the two strongest fortresses of France. These immense strongholds have menaced the peace and security of Germany, particularly the former, and it is, therefore, deemed of the highest importance that they should be captured and remain in our permanent possession. A fair number of heavy siege-guns have already arrived before Strasbourg. The Prussian 24-pounders are excellent and very effective; they have a wide range, and as soon as the distance has been correctly ascertained (which is generally the case after two or three trial shots), their fire is as accurate and telling as can be reasonably desired. In regard to Strasbourg, it would not be wise to calculate upon an immediate capitulation. General Uhlrich, the commander of the fortress, was formerly in the

Imperial Guard, and is an officer of the highest military ability, one who will do his duty to the last, and without any particular regard for the inhabitants of the city he is called upon to defend. I became personally acquainted with him at Varna, during the Crimean war, when we passed our leisure time in conversing about military matters, drinking a glass of light Brussa wine, and playing a game of dominoes. I remember well enough that we repeatedly touched on the possibility of our confronting each other as enemies. The brave general did not then imagine that the strongest army which the Second Empire could bring into the field would be repeatedly beaten by us within a fortnight, and that we could so soon commence the siege of the two most important French fortresses. The idea that the Germans would carry the war into French territory seemed too preposterous to the French, who thought it an easy task to drive the Prussians beyond the Rhine, and never expected to meet any serious resistance until they would reach Mayence and Coblentz. All their preparations show that this was their preconceived plan.

But to return to the siege of Strasbourg. Although the commander is a man of undoubted talent, energy, and bravery, and although the garrison is composed of select troops, who will fight and defend the city to the last, I do not believe this fortress will prove another Sebastopol. The numerous population of the city, amounting to more than 80,000 inhabitants, will be a serious check to the powers of resistance and endurance of the garrison, and will necessitate a speedier capitulation than could otherwise be anticipated. It is more than probable that our repeatedly expressed opinion that large and populous cities are not fit places for fortresses will obtain additional confirmation ere long. The principal objection against them is the difficulty, or rather impossibility, of provisioning them for a long siege. Of what use are the strongest walls and a great number of guns, when once famine, with its appalling consequences, spreads among a population of 80,000 souls? and how can the most energetic commander prevent it, and protect his army against its demoralizing influence? It is utterly impossible.

We have read many reports about the immense fortifications around Paris, and had an occasion to examine these strongholds a few years ago, and we readily confess that they are formidable, and were so previous to the numerous additions and improvements which have recently been made. But what of that? If what we have said above holds good with a city of 80,000 people, how much more so in regard to a capital of nearly 2,000,000 inhabitants, and composed of such dangerous and heterogeneous elements as the population of Paris? Some of the Paris newspapers contain an account of the quantities of provisions which are said to be stored in that city, and pretend that the place is fully prepared for a siege of four months. We feel inclined to think that the figures on paper will not correspond with the amount of stores actually on hand, and we should not be at all surprised to find these statements equal in exaggeration and want of truth to the reports circulated about the strength of the French army, its armament, equipment, and fitness for field service. We think that by the time the three immense columns of the German army shall appear before Paris, all the braggadocio about the defence of that city to the last will have been silenced by sounder counsel and cooler judgment. It would be the climax of madness to attempt a defence of Paris under the existing circumstances.

THE END.

THE FRANCO

PRUSSIAN WAR.

THE MINISTRY OF THE FRENCH REPUBLIC.

M. GREVY.
ÉMANUEL CREMIEUX.
LÉON GAMBETTA.
JULES FAVRE.
PIERRE MAGNE.
GEN. TROCHU.
JULES SIMON.
ANDRÉ LAVERTUJON.